THE BREWING CLOUD

by KENNY GOULD

Published 2020

Printed in the United States of America

ISBN: 9798617252530

This is a work of fiction. All names, characters, incidents, and businesses in this book are fictitious. Any similarity to real persons or entities, live or dead, is coincidental and not intended by the author.

Editing by John Knight

Cover design by Ryan Hayes

Typesetting by Stewart A. Williams / stewartwilliamsdesign.com

Independently published by Kenny Gould. First paperback edition.

For more information, visit www.hopculture.com or www.kennygould.com.

Dedication

For my parents, Amy and Wayne Gould, and to
Rachel Falik, for always encouraging me to write.

Contents

Hops and Barley

Late one evening, Hops and Barley talked about love. "What does it mean, oh green one?" Barley asked, as he bobbed in the light breeze.

"Acceptance, my prickly friend," Hops said. She smoothed her bracts, the green plates overlapping around her ample waist. "Love means unconditional acceptance."

"Not passion?" Barley asked.

Hops noticed with a twinge of jealousy that he glanced toward the female barley stalks, who giggled and batted their eyelashes, to the one. "No," she said. "Passion rises and falls like the wind. Love runs steady, like the sun."

Barley squinted toward the horizon, where the setting sun turned the sky shades of russet and ochre. The grass smelled like rain and the cicadas had just begun their monotone dirge. "But surely even the sun stops shining eventually," he said. "Right?"

Hops said, "Yes. You're right. I suppose all stories end."

"I love you," Barley said, laughing.

"I love you, too."

The next day, several men arrived with scythes and cut down all the barley. "You're all that matters, Hops," Barley said, as they bundled him into a sheaf. "Always and forever. Nothing changes."

And Hops said, "Nothing changes," and closed her eyes.

Four months later, the men came for her, attaching a bottom cutter to a tractor that she heard rumbling toward the field even before the carnage began. Dust flew. Soil shook. Then she fell into a basket and lay still. She thought of Barley and felt calm. Someone turned her upside down and fed her into a rattling machine, which separated her from her vine. She heard the vine screaming as a series of blades turned it into mulch. Then she fell onto a belt and felt her leaves torn apart from her stem.

The end, she thought, as she baked against the floor of a warm room. Moisture evaporated from under her bracts. She dried, desiccated, dehydrated, and deformed. Nine hours passed, and the men moved her to a colder room, where the little moisture left spread evenly throughout her body.

In the days that followed, she underwent a hundred other processes, until she was turned into liquid and bottled. She watched it all calmly, as if the chopping and drying and boiling and dying happened not to her, but to a character in a distant story. *How silly this character acted,* she thought. *Pining for a happy life.* She knew that love wasn't justice, and yet, against all odds, she'd hoped.

"Barley," she whispered. "I love you."

Her voice floated through her liquid body, moving in a thousand tiny bubbles from the bottom of the bottle toward its tapered neck. And from deep within her, inside the fluid fabric of her being, she heard a voice she thought long lost: "Hops!" Someone giggled. "I love you, too."

True Love

From the outside, you'd never know The Crow's Nest was a neighborhood bar. It looked like a convenience store, with a sign over the door that read, "J + D Convenience, snacks, ice, and cigarettes." Even when you walked through the front door, the place was set up like a bodega, with a shelf of toiletries and a rack of chips—salt and vinegar, barbecue, cheddar and sour cream. There were packs of gum and household items like laundry detergent and glue.

But toward the back of the store, by the illuminated drink machine that put out pedestrian soda products, were steps heading to the basement. A sign on the wall said, "Employees Only," but everyone knew that was only a ruse. Beneath the convenience store was where the galaxy's best beer moved from tap to glass. This was The Crow's Nest.

Twenty-four taps of liquid gold; rarest bottles bought and sold. That was the bar's slogan. Each tap poured the best the Cloud had to offer, and their extensive can and bottle list was unsurpassed. Shelves behind the bar held the greatest collection of glassware anywhere on the Cloud. Behind the bar was a small door that led to an office—a room truly for employees only—as well as a party room that doubled as the bar's museum. The bar's owner, Corey Greenblatt, had built illuminated shadowboxes into the walls, and inside each one he kept the rarest selections on his bottle list, each carefully locked behind a pane of glass.

The party room was where Jonah Tua spent the majority of his free time. Jonah was a Cloud native, six feet four inches of hard-packed muscle, good looks, and athletic instinct. When he wasn't modeling, he sat at the corner table beneath a bottle of Dr. Wunder's *emily*, a chocolate and orange blossom stout that Dr. Wunder had made to commemorate the birth of his only daughter. Supposedly, it was the rarest bottle of beer in existence. The brewery had sent a single bottle to each of the ten bars that had carried Dr. Wunder's product when the brewery first opened. Five of the bottles had since been consumed, three had been sold, and one had been destroyed when the basement of Cliffside flooded. That left a single bottle of *emily*, which was being aged to perfection behind glass in The Crow's Nest.

Other than The Crow's Nest, Jonah maintained the most robust collection of bottles on the Cloud. He had everything—Alligator Brewing's *Sabretooth*, Brana Brewing's *Blue-Green Star*, Cloudship's *Breakfast of Champions*—but he didn't have *emily*. He wanted that bottle. He needed that bottle. He sat beneath with his fingers tapping the table and sweat beading on his forehead, not so much enjoying the hustle and bustle of the bar or the smell of warm popcorn but simply basking in *emily*'s presence. He might've tried to steal the bottle but he'd been friends with Corey since childhood, ever since they'd played football together as boys. So he contented himself with sitting near the bottle, staring at the bottle, lusting after the bottle, like any other normal man with a slightly more-obsessive-than-average collection.

But one day, Jonah's girlfriend left him and he snapped.

Gone was the easy-going smile that graced advertisements for the Cloud's best beers, gone were the soft hands that baked cookies for his neighbors. Without Holly, Jonah indulged in his basest impulses, drawing down his savings to buy beer after beer after beer that he never even drank. He drifted toward madness, which was how he ended up at his favorite seat at The Crow's Nest, prepared to do something incredibly stupid.

As soon as Simon, the bar's dishwasher, ducked out back for a smoke, Jonah followed. Simon was on the bar's back step, his dirty apron hanging between his knees and a cigarette dangling from his lips.

"The weirdo that's always staring at Corey's bottles," Simon said, looking up as Jonah approached. He flicked his cigarette and it skittered into the alley, trailing embers as it bounced once, twice, three times before coming to a stop against a trash can. He stood, prepared to head back into the bar. "Nope. See ya later."

"Stay where you are," Jonah said, his voice hard as black ice. To his surprise, and perhaps Simon's as well, the man stopped. "I need you to find a new job," Jonah continued. "You've got mine."

Simon scoffed bitterly. He reached into his belt and came out with a knife. It was about six inches long, the blade glinting in the alley's flickering light. "You think I'm scared of you?" he said, jabbing the knife toward Jonah. "You have no idea who I am. You don't know what I've done. Back on Earth, they called me—"

He didn't get further before Jonah punched him in the jaw. It was a quick jab, perfectly executed, and Simon didn't see it coming. He toppled backward, falling into the bags of trash beside the door, and his knife went the way of his cigarette, skittering further into the alley.

"Yeah, that's cool," Jonah said, bending to retrieve the knife. He turned it over in his hands. "I don't care how bad you were on Earth. I don't care how many children you scarred or how many puppies you drowned. You have my job." He wrapped one massive hand around the blade of the knife and the other around its hilt. With a bare twitch, he snapped the knife in half and tossed the pieces at Simon's feet.

"Freak," Simon muttered, brushing off a piece of hamburger bun that clung to his apron. Slowly, he got to his feet.

"Do we have an understanding?" Jonah said.

Simon cleared his throat, spat at Jonah's feet, and then turned and walked into the bar.

The next day, when a "Help Wanted" sign appeared on the window of the Crow's Nest, Jonah was ready.

"Well, Jonah, I can't say I'm surprised to see you," Corey said, from behind his desk. His office was surprisingly sparse compared to the bar's orgy of light and color, little more than a broom closet with a desk, two chairs, and a couple of framed event posters. "You know I always want to support you, but is this a good idea?"

Jonah raised an eyebrow. He and Corey had met in high school when Corey's family had moved from Earth; Jonah was a linebacker on the football team and he'd taken Corey under his wing. Doubtless the lanky and bookish Corey would've had a much different teenage experience without Jonah's patronage, and they both knew it. "I know we've been friends for years," Corey said. "I'm just trying to look out for your best interests."

Jonah nodded. Corey was rational. He needed to play this cool.

"I understand your concern," he said. "I know my . . . history presents a bit of a liability. But I'm done with all that. If you look at it from another angle, there's no one on the Cloud more knowledgeable about beer who isn't currently working in the industry. I think I'd be a tremendous asset."

Corey shrugged. "What the hell," he said. "Let's do it. You can't be worse than Simon. The guy smelled like cigarettes and stole five bottles of Vampire's Fiftieth Box from me."

Jonah started the next day, picking up loose glassware and making sure the tables stayed clear. When the bar shut down for the night, he closed the taps and washed glassware, cleaned the bathrooms and mopped the floors. He'd been working at The Crow's Nest for a week before he made his move. It was 2:00 in the morning after a busy shift, and he and Corey were the only ones left in the bar. Jonah was scrubbing the bar while Corey filled out a chalkboard with the next day's draught selections.

"Hey Corey, if you ever wanted me to dust inside the cases, I'm happy to help," Jonah said. "You know, in your museum? I've noticed the bottles look a little dusty and I think they could use a good wipe."

Silence. Jonah looked up at Corey. For a moment, Jonah thought he'd overplayed his hand. Then Corey's face softened and he laughed.

"Oh no," he said. "I learned my lesson with Simon. Gave him a key on day one and bottles started going missing." He shook his head. "Once I make a rule for myself, I keep it. Three months before an employee gets a key to the bottles.

That's what I told myself. As a businessman, you're damned if you can't follow your own rules."

Jonah glanced toward *emily*. He couldn't help himself. Luckily, Corey was staring down at the chalkboard and didn't notice.

"Not a problem," Jonah growled. "Just thought I could help."

That evening, when Jonah got home, he punched a hole through his living room wall. Jonah had lost his girlfriend for that bottle. He'd made a man leave his job. Heck, he'd spent a week as a dishwasher. He took a deep breath, massaging his bloody knuckles. When had he gotten so mad over a bottle? This was silly. This was crazy! But—he had to remind himself—this wasn't any bottle. This was *emily*. Dr. Wunder's *emily*. Wars had been fought over less. If his sacrifices meant getting his hands on that bottle, it'd all be worth it. If he could rub his fingers over that label, he could be redeemed.

So for three months Jonah worked diligently and when the date arrived, Corey called him into the office.

"Well Jonah, I've been quite impressed," he said. "Honestly, you've done a terrific job. You're a model employee. Congratulations."

He flicked his wrist and something shiny tumbled through the air. Jonah caught it. It was a key, small and simple and perfect. He cradled the treasure in one hand and rubbed his thumb along the grooves. He could scarcely breathe.

"Thank you," he said.

That afternoon, when Corey ducked into the bathroom, Jonah slipped into the museum. He fished the key out of his pocket and dipped it into the lock that secured *emily*. With trembling fingers, he gave it a turn.

It didn't budge.

"Damn it," Jonah hissed. He glanced at bathroom door and jiggled the key in the lock, but it still didn't turn. Clearly, it was the wrong key. With a grunt of frustration, he took the key out of the lock and moved onto the next case, which opened without a problem. It was filled with a comparably average Green Smoke *Zazzle*—one of the rarest beers on the Cloud, but not *emily*. He began dusting right as Corey came out of the bathroom.

"Looks good, Jonah," Corey said. "You've been working hard."

"Of course," Jonah said. "Say, I was trying to dust the *emily*, but I couldn't get the case open. Is it broken or something?"

Corey laughed. "Not at all. But you know *emily*. It's the rarest beer on the Cloud." He patted his chest and Jonah saw the outline of something beneath his shirt. "I trust you, Jonah, but I don't trust anyone when it comes to that little lady. That one is kept behind bulletproof glass, and the walls of the case are six inches of hard steel. I don't let the key out of my sight."

Jonah forced himself to smile. "Understandable," he said. Then, before he could give it a second thought, he rushed Corey with a linebacker's speed, wrapping both arms around his waist and putting him on the ground. The two men wrestled, but Jonah was twice Corey's size. The former kicker didn't stand a chance.

"What are you doing?" Corey gasped, as Jonah fumbled with the front of his shirt. "Get off me."

When Jonah couldn't get Corey's shirt open, he simply ripped it with both hands, revealing a golden key on a chain that hung against Corey's chest. With a tug, Jonah snapped the chain and slipped the key into his palm.

"Stay where you are," he said, his voice hoarse. "I'm so sorry, Corey. I can't help myself. But if you come after me, I'll have to hurt you."

Quickly, he darted into the museum and slipped the key into *emily*'s lock. This time, the case swung open. Jonah took the bottle in his hands, allowing himself a moment of pure, unadulterated bliss before his eyes narrowed.

"Jonah, stop," Corey called from the other room, but Jonah was off, his old football instincts kicking in as he tucked the bottle protectively under one arm and pounded up the steps. A tourist stood near the drink fridge and Jonah pushed him over, sending him toppling into the chips. He hit the door at a sprint, the metal yielding before him as he burst into the bright afternoon.

Off to See the Wizard

ere's what I know about Dr. Gustav Wunder.
As an undergraduate senior at The Institute on Mars,
Dr. Wunder picked up a dog-eared copy of *Out of This Galaxy Home Brewing* and brewed his first beer. On the advice of a friend, he entered it into a local competition. When the beer won a first prize ribbon, Wunder focused his last two semesters on brewing, even writing his senior paper on the effects of atmosphere on mixed-culture fermentation.

Post-college, Wunder spent nine months working at a beer and wine making shop near the Institute. Then, he bought a ticket to the Brewing Cloud. His plan was to work for Gregor Eliot, the famed (late) owner of Crystal Tree Brewery. He walked in, ordered a beer, and told Gregor, "I've got everything I own in this suitcase and I moved here to work for you. I'll do any job you have if you'll help me learn about brewing."

Within a year, Wunder was the Head Brewer of Crystal Tree. Two years later, Wunder borrowed the money to open his own place. The original Wunder's Pub and Brewery was a sixty-seat brewpub in on the north side of the Cloud, near the Promenade. It opened to a packed house. From his seven-barrel basement brewery, Dr. Wunder crafted the beers that supplied the taps upstairs. Among his revolving offerings, an IPA called *Wet* attracted more attention than the others; restaurant workers often found patrons in the bathroom, illegally filling up plastic bottles so they could take the beer home.

Because of *Wet*'s success, Wunder planned to open a production facility. But just three days before the fifteen-barrel brewery was scheduled to open, the site caught fire. Many suspected arson, though nothing was ever proven. On what should've been the greatest day of his career, Dr. Wunder shuttered the doors to Wunder's Pub and Brewery and left the Cloud.

After that, no one knows exactly what happened to Gustav Wunder. For years he disappeared, and no journalist, private detective, or old friend managed to uncover anything about his whereabouts. Until one day, a new operation surfaced on the Cloud, a gigantic brewery behind high brick walls topped with silver spikes. Whispers went around the Cloud, but it wasn't until the day before the new brewery's steam stacks started belching that a sign appeared on the gate: Dr. Wunder's Magical Medicinal Brewery and Beer Emporium.

From the very beginning, it was clear this was an entirely different operation than the brewpub. In fact, they were so different it didn't even seem like they'd been started by the same person. For one, the scale was wholly different. At the Brewpub, Dr. Wunder made each batch himself, but that hardly seemed possible with the size of his new facility. And yet, while the scale had dramatically increased, so had the quality. The Brewpub made technically excellent beer, but the product that came out of Dr. Wunder's Magical Medicinal Brewery and Beer Emporium was simply incredible. It was—as the name suggested—almost magical. A single sip turned even stalwart skeptics into believers and evangelizers.

The effect on the Brewing Cloud can't be overstated. Always a popular destination among those who loved beer, it suddenly became a mainstream tourist attraction. People flooded to the Cloud, as did their money. For the first time since it was built, the Cloud saw a population increase. There were new shops, new buildings, new breweries. In Earth parlance, Dr. Wunder's transformed the Cloud from a one-horse, podunk town into New York City.

As a journalist, when I see money changing hands, I ask questions. Everyone knows that Dr. Wunder doesn't appear in public. In fact, I've been able to confirm that no one has seen the man in twenty years, not since the day he shuttered his original taproom. The gates to his brewery remained locked. No one goes in and no one comes out. What is he hiding?

Most recently, Dr. Wunder made the news by announcing that he's giving away five of his Rare Recipes. It was a stunning publicity play, but again, as a journalist, I feel a responsibility to play devil's advocate. At this point, with Dr. Wunder's current scale, he has more money than god. Besides the obvious publicity play, what does he gain with this stunt? Is it simply a play for more sales, or is there something else happening, something going on behind the scenes?

After three decades of this work, I've learned to trust my gut, and my instinct tells me that the story doesn't add up. When Dr. Wunder's original facility burned down, he didn't take the insurance money to build a new one. Instead, he shuttered the doors of his original, extremely popular brew-pub and left. Why? He could've continued to run the brew-pub. He could've rebuilt. But he disappeared for twenty years. Then he reappeared with a project that transformed the Cloud overnight, and he still hasn't shown his face.

What actually happened on that night the production facility burned down? Where did Dr. Wunder go? Why did he open the Magical Medicinal Brewery and Beer Emporium, and what's the impetus behind his latest publicity stunt?

There's a mystery here, and one that I'm determined to solve.

—*Alistair Gray, Journalist, Hop Culture*

Vampire Brewing

From the cracked door of her closet office, Meghan Campbell watched the man at the end of her bar.

"What do you think he wants?" she asked her marketing intern. Emily Wunder was a bit moon-eyed but savvy, with a terrific track record of making solid memes and handling online trolls. And it didn't hurt that her father ran Wunder's Pub and Brewery, the most successful brewery on the Cloud.

"It's been three days now, right?" Emily said. "Maybe he just likes beer."

Meghan shook her head. She'd had fans before, but this was wrong. The man just sat at the end of the bar and spoke to no one. During his time at Vampire, he'd ordered everything on the menu, starting with the first beer and working his way down the list. He wore a green cowl like he belonged to some coven of warlocks, the great hood shrouding his face. Three days and Meghan still had no idea what he looked like.

"I'm going to talk to him," Meghan said. "Wish me luck."

"I'll be waiting with the pepper spray," Emily said. "Yell if you need me."

Meghan walked into the taproom, feigning nonchalance as she ran a rag along the bar. This early in the afternoon, the bar was empty save for the hooded man, though Meghan had to admit it probably wasn't the time keeping people away. Of late, the taproom had been sadly empty, the result of being a legacy brewery in a market that valued experience over consistency. Most drinkers were too busy going crazy over Cloudship or Brana Brewing to visit her ten-year-old taproom. Usually, it was only her and Emily.

"You enjoying that brown ale?" Meghan said to the man, as goosebumps prickled her neck. He nodded once, the glass of beer disappearing into his oversized hood.

"Some weather we're having," she said. "Heat wave like I haven't seen in years. You from here?"

"Meghan Campbell." The man's voice was like gravel. "I know you dreamt of a place where people loved and laughed. You don't have it. But it doesn't have to be this way." He took a sip of the brown ale. "I represent Champagne Equities. I've come to make you an offer."

The man placed a stack of papers on the bar, as well as a letter opener. The handle of the opener was polished elk horn and the blade was silver.

"This is a contract. A signature, and you'll have success. I invite you to read the offer and see what you think."

Meghan picked up the elk-horn opener and then dropped it back on the contract.

"What's this? I prick my finger and sign in blood? Because those are the kind of vibes you're giving off."

From within his hood, the man laughed. It was cold, without any humor.

"Of course not," he said. "This is simply a gift. To celebrate our future success."

Something slapped against the front of the building. The sky had darkened and the weather was turning. The wind charged the leaves into a frenzy. The wind churned the leaves into a frenzy.

"I'll think about it," she said, taking the contract and the letter opener. "You need another beer? We're closing soon."

The man drained the last of his ale. "Actually, I was just leaving," he said.

When the man was gone, Meghan locked the front door and leaned against it. Her heart pounded. She glanced over the first few pages of the contract—it was a boilerplate buyout, though there was also some strange language about "taking the success of another."

Meghan sighed and headed back into the office.

"He wanted a date, didn't he?" said Emily, without looking up from her computer. She was making a flyer for an upcoming release. Little fruits danced around text. "You should put me in charge sometime. Go have some fun."

Emily dropped her opener and the contract on the desk. "I'm not putting a fifteen-year-old in charge of my taps," she said. "He wanted to make a deal."

Emily turned. "What kind of deal?" she asked.

"Oh, the usual. I give up equity and they control my brand and trademarks. And I steal the success of someone else. Or something."

Emily raised an eyebrow. "Did he say where he was from?"

"Champagne Equities."

Emily shook her head. "You don't want that," she said. "Champagne is wrong. They're evil."

Meghan felt a righteous anger. For one brief moment, from the corner of her eye, she swore she saw the blade of the elk horn opener glint.

"What do you know about it?" she said, fixing her gaze on Emily. "You're in high school. You think this is fun for me? Stressing day after day about how I'm going to pay rent? There's a reason I haven't been on a date in years. This is the most miserable I've ever been in my life."

She breathed heavily. She lifted the letter opener for comfort and tucked it into her belt.

"I'm sorry," Emily mumbled. "It's just . . . They approached my father, too. They're not good people, Meghan. You might not have the success you want, but you've got your pride. Your freedom. Champagne will take that away."

Meghan felt the walls closing around her. This time, she felt the blade of the opener grow warm against her waist.

"Of course, the fifteen-year-old daughter of the man with the most popular brewery on the Cloud is telling me how to run my business. Why are you here, Emily Wunder? You spying on me? You come to laugh?"

Emily looked horrified. "Not at all," she said. "I believe in Vampire. I thought I could help."

"Get out," Meghan said, sweeping open the office door. "Leave, and don't come back. Your internship is over."

When the man in the cowl returned, the bar was empty.

"Have you made up your mind?" he asked.

Meghan handed him the contract. "Signed," she said. "I'm ready for success."

The man bowed. For the first time, Meghan saw part of his face. It was just the lower half, from the nose down, but he was smiling. He had a mouth full of perfectly white teeth.

"Now the fun can begin," he said.

From beneath his cowl, the man drew a suitcase and

flipped the latches. Inside were twelve different bottles of beer.

"Whose success will you take?" he asked.

Meghan still didn't understand what he was asking, but she pointed to the purple and yellow label of a beer from Wunder's Pub and Brewery.

"That one," she said. "I want his success."

It was fifteen years later and late afternoon when Meghan celebrated Vampire's 25th Anniversary. While she waited for her guests, she opened her mail with an elk horn opener. She brushed her hair behind an ear; of late, it had been turning gray.

Meghan glanced at her watch and then at the keg of Fiftieth Box behind the bar. The beer was aged in whiskey barrels atop smoked applewood chips. It was her most famous beer, the one that the brewery sold for sixty dollars per bottle.

She opened another letter. Where was everyone? In the days before Champagne, the brewery had occupancy for thirty-four people, and another eight in the cellar. The lights down there hardly worked, and a pink-toed tarantula lived in the dark space just above doorway at the bottom of the steps. It never bothered Meghan, but every time that prissy Emily Wunder had peered at the doorway too long, it would poke out a hairy leg and make her scream.

Champagne had renovated her taproom, turned it into a state-of-the-art concert venue with occupancy for three hundred and fifty. They'd hired a local artist to cover the walls with interpretations of her products. The Fiftieth Box was done with vivid colors and exaggerated dimensions; Bowie

Knife was a mosaic made up of chips from actual knife blades. Champagne had added windows, a hundred panes of glass, all etched with the Vampire logo. If she stood in the tap room and looked down, she could see her barrel room. Below that, birds, clouds, and miles of bright blue sky.

And yet, the taproom had been open for three hours and no one had come to celebrate.

Even as Meghan started to feel sorry for herself, the door opened and a kindly-looking man entered the bar. He wore blue jeans and a flannel shirt, and looked like someone's well-meaning grandfather.

"Hello," she said, setting the elk-horn opener on the table. "Welcome to the twenty-fifth anniversary. Can I get you a drink?"

The old man's gaze wandered through the taproom, over the contemporary furniture, embossed windows, and long bar, coming to a rest on the tap handles that stuck out of a metal sculpture of a bat in flight. His eyes settled on Meghan.

"What is this?" he asked.

"You're in Vampire Brewing," Meghan said. "Most distributed brewery in the galaxy. Home of the famed Fiftieth Box. A drink?"

The man turned around and glanced at the door. "Isn't this Green Smoke?"

"This is Vampire," she said. "Green Smoke Brewing is down the street."

The man left. Anger rose within Meghan, cold and righteous, and her grip tightened around the elk horn opener. The handle quivered, and Meghan saw that she'd driven the blade half an inch into the wood.

Not for the first time, Meghan thought about her brewery's namesake and wondered why people hated him. Dracula gave others power; he gave them eternal life. For that, they turned against him.

Meghan removed the blade from the table and scratched at the divot with her thumbnail. She looked at the brewery's double doors: they needed more character. Maybe she'd go after them with the letter opener. If anyone asked about the strange scrapes, she'd say that the doors had once kept Dracula trapped inside a room, and that the rents were the places where the poor beast scratched his nails bloody against the wood, trying to get out.

The Skeleton

A nne pressed her foot against the base of a shovel, the blade cutting into the dry earth. She tossed the dirt into a growing pile and went back for another load. And another. A pit slowly took shape, the perfect hole in which to drive a stake. The stake would form the base of the trellis that would hold up the vines, and hopefully she could control the farm for three years until the first crop. It was a pipe dream, but what else could she do? Her pappy had worked this land, and his pappy before him, and so on, and she'd throw herself over the Cloud's nearby edge before she gave up his dream of a hundred acres—or, worse yet, give anything to the bank that, of late, had become increasingly persistent.

That thought kept Anne working, even as the sun set and the shovel rubbed new blisters into her hands. Despite the hardships, she loved her land, and the tough but simple life it afforded. But there was only so much work even Anne Westing could handle in a day. She was about to break for the evening when she saw something sticking from the dirt at the bottom of the pit. She set down the shovel and jumped in, dropping to her hands and knees and brushing loose soil away. She gasped. It was a skull. She didn't know what kind, but it didn't belong to a human. The triangular sockets stared accusingly at the woman who dared disturb the skull's slumber, the upturned mouth of leonine molars a channel for the wind. When it was alive, the creature had clearly possessed a snout, and tusks, and either a horn or a third eye, right in the middle of its forehead. Anne didn't have a formal education, but she'd seen Fenemas around the Cloud, their thick skin and multiple legs making them look like giant lizards. There were Zorgans, with their translucent metal skulls and chests full of wires, and Yirkutskans, humanoid save for their bugs eyes and swishing tails. But none of them looked anything like this. Even further out, where she'd heard rumors of Cramptons and Treelees, she didn't know of anything that looked like this.

Anne dug deeper into the dirt with her chipped fingernails, revealing neck bones, a breastplate, and long, spindly arms. She dug further, finding finger bones clutched around a green bottle. Remarkably, the glass was unbroken, the cork stopper still secured with a tight wire hood. Age had marred the label, though she made out the faint swirls of an alien language. There was a picture of the creature that must have been similar to the one she'd found, though this one had pink skin, and—yes—a third eye.

What was this creature? And what had it been holding? She lifted the bottle from the dirt and held it to the weakening sun. There was liquid inside, filled to a half inch below the cork. Was this an alien beer? She didn't know. She looked back down at the skeleton and tried to piece together how the creature had died. The skull was in excellent condition and didn't look like it had sustained any trauma. Perhaps it was from another planet and its biology didn't agree with the Martian air? But if that were the case, where was the creature's ship?

Her eyes fell on the field beside her. She shook her head. No way. Nope. She wasn't digging up her family farm on the hunch that some alien ship might be buried deep beneath it. She didn't have time and if she found something, the farm would be swarmed by all sorts of weirdos. Scientists, government officials, conspiracy theorists. They'd quarantine her land and send her to some lightless cell, where she'd be pressed, prodded, and interrogated twelve kinds of sideways. All the while, people would be trampling her soil, their fingers poking her plants, their dirty hands covering her crops with chemicals and barraging her hops with a battery of tests and assays. Who'd buy crop from someone suspected of harboring aliens? The taint of the spectacle alone would destroy her.

Carefully, calmly, Anne brushed dirt back over the skeleton. The bottle . . . well, it'd look nice above her mantle. She climbed out of the pit, lifted her shovel, and headed back toward the house.

The Westing residence was a shell of Anne's former home, three quarters of the rooms empty save for dust and spiders. The cracked hardwood went unpolished and paint peeled from the outer walls, little chips falling off every time someone slammed the door. If the bank ever came for her estate, the house would be the first thing she'd let go, though she doubted she'd get much for it.

Behind the house was an aging barn with a leaky roof where Anne kept her tools. By the time she'd put away her shovel, set the mysterious bottle on the mantel, and washed up, her helper Simon had dinner ready, two bowls of steaming lentils seasoned with whatever they had in the pantry.

Lately, that wasn't much. But she took a seat at the table and dug in, the smell making her mouth water.

They ate in silence. Like her, Simon was quiet by nature, though she suspected it was because he was trying to hide a dangerous past. Still, he worked hard and Anne couldn't run the farm by herself. When he'd shown up at the beginning of the year, looking for work in exchange for room and board, she didn't think twice about taking him in. His scars might've given another pause, but Anne could handle herself. She'd dealt with wild hogs, beer roaches, and bankers. She could deal with Simon.

That night, as she lay in bed and listened to the wind howl outside her window, she thought of her childhood, of the busy house and bustling farm and holidays with tables full of steaming food and presents. In those days, it didn't seem like anything could go wrong. What had happened? It had become cheaper to import hops than to grow them. Never mind the quality. Her siblings and cousins found better opportunities elsewhere, and then it was just her living alone on her family's land. She stared at the ceiling and finally drifted off.

Anne woke with the sun and dressed quickly. The water to the house had been shut off two months before, but one of Simon's responsibilities was to keep the bucket on her dresser filled with clean water. Anne had just splashed a bit of the cool liquid on her face when she heard him calling from downstairs.

"Anne? Anne, come down here, quickly."

Anne went downstairs to find Simon standing in the living room, his mouth open and his face pale. Anne followed his gaze to the bottle on the mantle. It was exactly where

Anne had left it, except that the liquid inside was glowing a bright, almost blinding blue.

"What is that?" Anne asked, looking curiously at the bottle. "What did you do?"

"I didn't do anything," Simon said, his voice gruff. "I came in here and it was glowing like that. Where did it come from?"

Anne was about to answer when someone knocked at the door. She looked at Simon, his mouth open and his eyes wide. Slowly, she approached the old wooden door and put a hand on the brass knob. She pulled. Standing on the porch was a tall man in a black suit. He had a slick handlebar mustache and jet black hair covered with gel and combed to one side. Behind him, a long black car idled on the rocky path. Standing beside the car was a photographer and a woman inappropriately dressed in a rhinestone bra and fez with a tassel.

"Are you Anne Westing?" the man on the porch said, and his voice was that of a backcountry auctioneer. Without waiting for her to answer, he said, "Well, well, well, do I have a surprise for you. I have the distinct honor of presenting you with the Wunder Award for Cloud's Most Dynamic Agricultural Product."

He handed her a certificate. Anne scanned it quickly. It was one of those elaborate pieces of paper with a dubious amount of meaning.

"You're an award-winning farmer," the man said, grabbing Anne's hand and pumping it furiously. He had a gold bracelet that bounced and jangled with the motion. Just when Anne thought her arm would break, he stood to the side so the photographer could see her as he snapped pictures.

"Congratulations. The award comes with a five-thousand-dollar stipend that I now present to you in the form of this gigantic novelty check."

The woman in the fez came up the stairs holding the check.

"Smile now," the man said, moving to the side so the photographer could get her in the picture. "Smile, and congratulations again. I'm sure you have extremely dynamic product."

He bowed before following the woman with the fez down the porch steps and into the black car that waited for them. The photographer had already climbed inside. The engine roared and the car spat a cloud of dust, moving back down the path as quickly as it had arrived.

"What just happened?" Simon asked, as Anne closed the door.

"It seems I won an award for having dynamic agricultural product," Anne said. She leaned the novelty check against the wall and placed the certificate on the table beside the door. "And got five thousand dollars."

Simon glanced toward the mantle. "Do you think it has anything to do with . . . that?"

Anne looked back to the bottle. It had stopped glowing and looked like a simple 750 milliliter bottle with a tight wire hood and liquid inside, filled to a half inch from the cork. And alien writing on the label.

"I'm not sure," she said. "It is an odd coincidence."

"Where'd you say you got that?" Simon asked.

Anne shrugged. "I didn't say. But I'll level with you. I was out in the field, digging holes for the new plants, when I came across a skeleton. It didn't look like anything I'd ever seen and it was holding that." She pointed to the bottle. "I thought about telling someone but I think it could only do more harm than good, so I put the skeleton back in the ground and kept this bottle as a little keepsake."

"You found an alien skeleton in your field and you just buried it?"

Again, Anne shrugged. "I don't know what else to do. I got enough to worry about. Though I have to say, this check comes at a very strange time. Looks like I can delay the bank for another month. If only there was another zero on the end, we could repay that loan and we wouldn't have to worry about anything."

"That's not strange to you?"

Anne glanced at the check. It did seem odd that she'd find the skeleton and win a check in the same twenty-four-hour period. She'd never heard of the Wunder Award for Cloud's Most Dynamic Agricultural Product, but five thousand dollars would go a long way toward improving the quality of her life.

"Nothing to do for it," Anne said.

"The bottle is glowing again," Simon said. Anne followed his gaze to the bottle, which now glowed a neon green. "Can I see the skeleton?"

Anne shook her head. "Should of left that bottle in the field," she said. "I'll bury it back today. We got work to do and we don't have time for fooling around."

Simon rolled his eyes. "Come on," he said. "It's not every day you find an alien skeleton and get a mystery check for five thousand big ones. Live a little. You can take ten minutes to show me the skeleton. Besides, you said you wanted to bury the bottle."

Anne sighed. "All right," she said. "Come on. And grab that thing. I'll get the shovel from the shed."

Anne got the shovel and led Simon through the field to the dig site. It was as it had been the day before, a small pit with dirt brushed over the bottom to cover the skeleton.

"Take your look and then hop out, because I have stakes to install," Anne said, driving the shovel into the earth. "And a damn distracting bottle to get rid of."

Simon smirked. "So serious," he said. He pointed to the pit. "What, it's down there?" Anne nodded. Simon jumped down and brushed dirt away from the pit's bottom. He whistled.

"Look at this," he said. "I've never seen anything like that. Not in all my travels. Triangular eyes? It almost doesn't look real. And check this out."

He moved to the side to reveal something Anne hadn't seen: a suitcase, made of silver metal, embedded in the ground near the skeleton's outstretched fingers. Anne shook her head. That couldn't be. She'd been kneeling right where Simon was now, her hands moving dirt exactly where the suitcase now lay. But she hadn't seen a thing.

"Did you see this?" Simon asked. His hands brushed the case and it popped open with a hiss, making him yell and stumble away. "My god," he said. The case was filled with cash.

"Don't touch that," Anne said, but Simon was already on top of it, counting the thick stacks of money.

"There's a thousand dollars here," Simon said, holding up a wad of twenty dollar bills. He grabbed another stack and held it up to the first. "And this one is the same size." He dropped both stacks and used his pointer finger to count the piles in the suitcase. "Eight stacks, five rows. There's forty-five thousand dollars in here."

The immensity of the sum hit Anne just before she realized the significance. The five thousand dollars she'd won through an award she'd never heard of, plus the forty-five thousand in the mysterious suitcase, was the exact amount she needed to repay the bank. All received in a single morning. All received the day after she'd found the skeleton.

"We're rich," Simon said. "You can pay off the bank. That's fifty thousand. The exact amount you need. Who knows what else will come from this?"

"Get out of the pit, Simon," Anne said.

"Don't you see?" Simon said. "That bottle is a good luck charm of sorts. It's like an alien rabbit foot. All of our problems are solved."

Anne lifted the shovel from the ground and leveled the blade at him. "Out of the pit."

Simon met Anne's gaze, his brown eyes burning, but he climbed out of the pit.

"You're not thinking straight," he said. "Your prayers have been answered and you're not going to take advantage of that? I got a rap sheet on Earth with more crimes than you could count. Maybe that bottle can help me clear my name."

"You don't get something for nothing," Anne growled. "There's always a price to pay. Until I see the side effects of that bottle, I'm not using it."

"You want to live on this awful farm, go right ahead," Simon said. "But I want to clear my name. I want to be rich."

Anne shook her head. "This awful farm has been in my

family for generations," she said. "I like it here. I'm locking that thing away. Go home and start making lunch."

Simon looked at Anne, and then he grabbed the bottle.

"No," she said, but he was already running. "Simon, come back."

Anne was tall, taller than Simon, and each step carried her further, but Simon had adrenaline on his side. He ran like a man possessed, glancing back every few steps. The bottle, clutched in his left hand, had started glowing red.

"Stop," Anne called. "You don't understand what you're doing. Stop!"

The ground, wet from the evening's rain, was slippery. Too slippery to be running top speed on a rocky path at the edge of the Cloud, where a single wrong move could send one tumbling into oblivion.

"Simon," she called. "Slow down."

But it was too late. Simon, almost to the main road, glanced back one last time, and then his feet were out from under him. The glowing bottle tumbled out of his hand and came to a stop in a tangle of roots along the Cloud's edge. But Simon wasn't so lucky. He grasped at the roots, missed, and then he was over the edge. Anne ran to the side in time to see his flailing form vanish into a puffy white cloud. Then, he was gone.

Anne lifted the bottle. It had stopped glowing. She sighed and tucked it into her back pocket, and then she walked back toward the dig site. She had hops to plant.

The Spacedogs Visit the Brewing Cloud

Several miles above the Brewing Cloud, in a ship splattered with the bright green image of a three-headed dog, sat the universe's most famous band.

"Four minutes, thirty-seven seconds," said the pilot. His friends called him Captain Robot; he played bass.

"I'm so glad I escaped this place," said Mr. Smooth, the band's lead singer. He was a handsome man with skin the color of beach sand and thick muscles that stretched the fine fabric of his dress shirt. He glanced out the cockpit window. "It stinks out here. And the women are so ordinary. Not like our darling Metal Werewolf."

At the sound of her name, Metal Werewolf looked up from where she napped with Bageera, the band's guitarist, on a pad in front of a large instrument console. Bageera was a sentient panther from some far off corner of the galaxy. Metal Werewolf was a metal werewolf. She growled and bared her teeth.

"Oh hush, Jonah," Bageera said, licking his right paw. "Panther, person, it doesn't matter. Remember who you were before I brought you into this band."

Mr. Smooth rolled his eyes. "Whatever," he said. "It's not like I have family here anymore. Honestly, this place sucks. We're in, we're out. Let's go back to Venus."

Captain Robot swiped at Mr. Smooth's feet. "Get those down," he said. "You almost hit the ejector seat."

"I know exactly what I'm doing," said Mr. Smooth, but he took his feet down. "At least they'll have good beer," he said, and crossed his arms.

As the ship settled onto the dock, a metal ramp extended from the door to the ground. Mr. Smooth heard the roaring crowd and tried to peer through the smoke that obscured the gangplank.

"Music to my ears," he said, rubbing his hands together. Beside him, Metal Werewolf growled something.

"What was that?" he said, looking down at her. "Yes, I know they like me. Doesn't mean I have to like them."

Mr. Smooth stepped through the smoke to embrace the applause and shouts of adoration he heard recycled from other platforms throughout the galaxy. "That's nice of them," he said as he looked over a sea of people barely contained by metal barriers and security personnel. "I think that—"

A woman reached toward him. A Yirkutskan—he could tell by the shimmering tattoos that ran up both her arms. She flashed a smile, showing her tiny white teeth, each sharpened to a point. A long tail curled around her waist.

"My god," he exclaimed. "You're beautiful."

"Please stay back, Mr. Smooth," one of his bodyguards said, getting between him and the Yirkutskan. "We need to get you inside."

"Never mind that," Mr. Smooth said, trying to glimpse the woman. He imagined the seductive flick of her tail. "Out of my way."

He pushed past the guard but the Yirkutskan was gone.

"Damn it," he hissed. Behind him, Bageera and Metal Werewolf signed autographs. Mr. Smooth ignored them, heading straight for the first of two black vehicles that idled just inside the row of protective barriers. He climbed into the back and shut the door.

"Drive me to the hotel," Mr. Smooth said, pulling off his sunglasses.

"You want to wait for the others?" The driver glanced at him in the rearview mirror.

"Now."

In his room, Mr. Smooth sulked.

"I need to find that woman," he said, driving a fist into a pillow.

Someone knocked on the door.

"I'm busy," Mr. Smooth said. A moment passed, and the knock came again. "I'm busy!" When the knock came again, Mr. Smooth threw open the heavy door. Instead of Captain Robot, or one of his bodyguards, he saw the Yirkutskan.

"Hi," she said, shyly. "One of your bodyguards said you were looking for me. Can I come in?"

Two hours later, Mr. Smooth sat with his back against the headboard, the Yirkutskan tracing circles on his bronze stomach with her index finger.

"That was terrific," he said, taking a drag on his cigarette. "Say, what do people do for fun around here?"

"I wouldn't know," the Yirkutskan said. "I'm not from here. I only came up for the contest."

"Ah," Mr. Smooth said. He'd seen the flyer in the elevator. Apparently some rich idiot named Dr. Wunder was giving away five of his secret beer recipes. The Cloud was going crazy for them. Mr. Smooth remembered a Wunder from his childhood, but he didn't remember him being a doctor, or being particularly wealthy. Maybe this was his son. Or daughter. He had to remember the times.

He was about to suggest they get back under the covers when the phone rang. Mr. Smooth shifted slightly and lifted the receiver.

"Jonah Tua," he said. "Can I help you?"

"Mr. Smooth," said the voice on the other end of the line. It was low and robotic, almost like the voice of Captain Robot. "Pleasure to have you back on the Cloud. We need a song from you. Now. Track the Captain to find us. Tell anyone about this and we'll kill him."

The line went dead.

For a moment, Mr. Smooth stared at the phone and then he shook off the Yirkutskan.

"Is everything okay?" she asked.

Mr. Smooth sighed. "I really hate this place," he said.

Mr Smooth had been kidnapped before. For whatever reason, people assumed a friendliness that he didn't reciprocate. Rich bastards—it was always rich bastards—captured him for innocuous events like birthday parties or weddings or because they wanted a song and figured he'd join the fun. And to be honest, most of the occasions hadn't been so bad. In fact, it almost became a game for fans to try and kidnap the handsome lead singer. He was the best man at a wedding on Saturn. He'd gotten a galactic limousine ride to Thogg. At the end of every kidnapping, he left hazy and happy, with new friends and memories dulled by the fuzzy glow of intoxication.

That was, until Kepler-78. On that fateful trip, he'd been brought to perform at a birthday party. When his team came to rescue him, the drunken host pulled a pistol, shooting one of his bodyguards through the heart. She was dead before she hit the ground. The host was dead a second later, knocked into a sea of magma—the birthday party had taken place inside an active volcano. Mr. Smooth had walked away from the ordeal, but he started taking kidnappings a lot more seriously.

However, this was the first time someone had tried to kidnap the Captain. There was reason for that—Captain Robot was a terrifying force, an old unit from the military campaign on Mars. On Thogg, when Mr. Smooth had been kidnapped by pirates, Captain Robot had eviscerated their enemies with his shoulder guns and tossed their bloody bodies into the Boiling Sea. On Saturn, when he'd been taken for ransom by a notorious intergalactic criminal, the Captain had used his chest rockets to level an entire neighborhood. On that fateful trip to Kepler-78 . . . well, Mr. Smooth didn't like to think about that. But the point was, Captain Robot was the strongest of them. If someone had kidnapped the Captain, Mr. Smooth thought it best to follow orders.

So for the next three hours, Mr. Smooth followed the blip on the screen of his phone through the streets of the Brewing Cloud.

"Extortionists," he hissed, as Captain Robot's tracking device led him through an alley. "Idiots. Wasters of time."

He checked his screen; the tracking software placed Captain Robot inside a nearby three-story townhouse. From across the street, it looked empty, just like all the houses on this street. Perhaps the locals were sleeping, or partying with the tourists closer to town.

As he stepped to the porch, something stung his neck. His fingers wrapped around the shaft of a small dart.

"Shit," he said, yanking the dart from his neck. Already he felt slow and sluggish, his floppy hands barely responding. He fell, the back of his head cracking against the concrete.

When Mr. Smooth awoke, he found himself on the floor of a fifteen-foot by fifteen-foot cubicle. There was a single window covered with a metal panel. A camera and speaker sat high in one corner. Slowly, he pushed himself to his feet and tried the door.

Locked.

He looked into the camera. "I'm not the only one with Captain Robot's tracking device," he said. "The Intergalactic Police also have the code."

No one responded. Perhaps they could see through the lie. He flashed a lewd gesture at the camera. When no one responded, he kicked the window. His ankle bent and he hopped around on one leg, clutching his foot.

"I never even wanted to come back here," he moaned.

He sat down and picked at the lint on his thigh. Perhaps at any moment, the Captain would blast through the wall, eyes flashing red and weapons online, as had happened on so many other occasions. But five minutes passed and nothing happened. Then twenty. Just as Mr. Smooth started to doze, a voice from the speaker said, "I'm sorry to have kept you."

Mr. Smooth sat up. The voice was low and robotic, clearly the same one from the phone in Mr. Smooth's hotel.

"Do you know who I am?" the voice said.

Mr. Smooth snorted. "I have no idea," he said. "Some fan with a little too much time on his hands. Say, why don't you let me out?"

For a moment, nothing happened, and then the voice said, "I need a song from you. An original song, for old times' sake."

Mr. Smooth shook his head. Everyone knew he didn't write music. He didn't even play an instrument. Or sing. Bageera had found him outside a meeting for recovering bottle collection addicts and recruited him solely for his looks. His vocals were pre-recorded by Bageera and synced to his lips with holo-film.

"You have an hour," the voice said.

"This is ridiculous," Mr. Smooth said. "You know I don't write our music, right? I'm just the front man. And if you didn't know, there's no way you have the Captain. He's a G-8 unit. There's no way he'd be captured by someone so uninformed."

A small port opened in the ceiling and a pen fell at Mr. Smooth's feet. Several sheets of paper floated after it.

"One hour."

Mr. Smooth sighed. He picked up the pen and paper. "Bugger off," he wrote. "Love, Mr. Smooth."

Captain Robot would save him. He always did. He sat back down and waited for the fireworks.

An hour later, Mr. Smooth awoke to the sound of metal sliding against metal.

"The cavalry has arrived," he said.

Only, it wasn't Captain Robot. Rather, the metal plates across his window were slowly retracting, revealing a warehouse. In the middle of the room, suspended from one foot above a steaming vat of wort, hung an unresponsive Captain Robot.

"Let's hear your song," the voice said from the speaker.

Mr. Smooth swallowed. What could he do? He launched into a passible rendition of "Ice Woman," one of the band's most popular songs.

"I wanted something original," the voice said. "Did I not make myself clear?"

Sweat broke out on Mr. Smooth's forehead. "We can work something out," he said.

"You have five minutes," the voice said.

The chain began lowering Captain Robot toward the vat.

"I don't write the songs," Mr. Smooth said. "I don't play any instruments. I'm the face. The front man! Bageera's the one you want. Or even Captain Robot. Wake him up. I'm a hack!"

No response.

"Okay, okay," Mr. Smooth said. He picked up the pen. "Think, Smooth. Roses are red, violets are blue, I want to kick you with my shoe. No! Four and twenty blackbirds, baked into—"

In frustration, he snapped the pen in half. The plastic shattered, spilling ink down one wrist. He stared at the splintered pieces.

"I can't do it," he said.

Mr. Smooth dropped the pieces of plastic. What had Bageera taught him? That to write a song, he needed to access his emotions? But that was the problem—he didn't have any. At least, not ones that he hadn't dulled with women, drugs, and booze. If only he had a bottle of whiskey.

"I need a cigarette and a woman," he said, trying to keep his voice from quivering. "A broken heart and the kiss of ash."

He glanced at the window. Captain Robot dangled a few feet above the vat.

"That's my song!" he said. "Stop the chain!"

But it didn't stop.

Mr. Smooth pounded his fist against the window. Captain Robot had been behind his transformation from heartbroken alcoholic to galactic star. He'd tutored him, supported him, saved him on numerous occasions. Seventeen times, Mr. Smooth had been kidnapped. Seventeen times, Captain Robot had rescued him. Mr. Smooth tried to remember the last words he'd spoken to his friend; he was pretty sure he'd told the Captain to screw off.

"I'm sorry, Robot," he said. He ran an ink-stained hand across his forehead. In that moment, he felt something he hadn't felt in a long time: feeling itself. He loved Captain Robot. He needed him. He felt appreciation for Captain Robot, and the other Spacedogs. And he felt anger. Real, unadulterated anger toward this person holding them hostage for some stupid love song. What selfishness!

"You terrible person," he growled. "Let me tell you something."

And Mr. Smooth sang.

When the door finally opened, Mr. Smooth jumped to his feet.

"You bastard," he said, as a figure stepped into the doorway. "How could you...?"

Mr. Smooth trailed off as he found himself staring down

the barrel of a pistol.

"Calm yourself, Jonah," said the man holding the pistol. He wore a forest green robe and cowl that shrouded his face. "You really have no idea who I am?"

Mr. Smooth shook his head. The man with the gun pulled aside the cowl, revealing the bottom half of his face. Mr. Smooth saw a smile filled with perfectly white teeth.

"I'm the richest person in the world," the man said. "But even money can't fix this."

The man let the cowl fall and Mr. Smooth saw his face. He gasped. The man had no hair. No eyebrows. His skin, red and raw, pulled tight against the tortuous ridges of his cheekbones. One eye was missing entirely, the socket little more than a black pit.

"You came to my party, all fun and games, and then you got drunk and pulled a gun," the man said, his good eye flashing. "Remember? Remember when you told Captain Robot to toss me into a river of fire?"

Mr. Smooth shook his head. That wasn't what had happened. Was it?

"Kepler-78," he said.

"Kepler-78," said the man, nodding in agreement. "There was no reason for violence. You brought that to my party. I only drew my weapon after you threatened me."

Mr. Smooth closed his eyes. Was that what had happened? He didn't trust his memories. When he drank, he got out of control. It was part of the reason he'd left the Cloud to begin with.

"So here we are," the man said, and Mr. Smooth opened his eyes. "And now you're free to go."

The man tucked the gun into a fold of his robe and

stepped aside, motioning Mr. Smooth into the hallway. Mr. Smooth raised a curious eyebrow.

"You're letting me go?" he said. "Just like that?"

The man pulled up his cowl and adjusted it until all Mr. Smooth could see were his shining teeth.

"Killing you would change nothing," the man said. "It's enough for me to know that I could. Goodbye, Mr. Smooth. Get out, before I change my mind."

Mr. Smooth wanted to tell the man that this seemed like a fairly stupid revenge, but he wisely held his tongue.

"And the Captain?"

"He's fine. Already back at the hotel."

Mr. Smooth stepped toward the door. The man made no move to stop him. "For what it's worth, I'm sorry about Kepler-78," he said. "I don't get so drunk anymore. I'm a different person now."

"So am I," the man said ominously, grinning as Mr. Smooth walked past him. "So am I."

Several miles above the Brewing Cloud, in a ship splattered with the bright green image of a three-headed dog, sat the universe's most famous band.

"Ten sold," Bageera said, laying down his cards.

"I see your ten with an eye pot," Captain Robot said, flipping a chip onto the table. "Smooth?"

"Ah, I'm sorry guys," Mr. Smooth said, turning back to the table. He'd been staring out the window. "I'm distract-ed." He turned a card at the end of the table. "Seven high. Looks like I lost. Again."

"Not like you," Captain Robot said, raking a pile of chips toward him. "Are you all right?"

Mr. Smooth glanced back out the window. Far beneath them, the lights of the Brewing Cloud's smokestacks disappeared beneath a cover of purple and ochre clouds. Somewhere down there was a man he'd wronged. A past he couldn't face.

"I'm fine," he said, sighing. "But let's not play here again."

Upside Down

I like this new selection," Holly Black said to Corey Greenblatt, the owner of her favorite bar. She swirled her glass of kettle sour flavored with a proprietary herb package. It had been aged for a month in gin barrels over organic parsnip and triple dry-hopped with lupulin powder. "But I think it tastes a lot like that other gin-aged sour you had on last week."

Corey continued wiping down the bar with a rag.

"There's no innovation in beer anymore," Holly lamented. "Maybe at Dr. Wunder's but good luck getting your hands on any of that. I think my tenure on the Cloud might be nearing its end."

Holly slouched, continuing to swirl the unsatisfying amber liquid around her tasting glass. She thought back to her first sip of craft beer, which had occurred at a party during her graduate studies on Venus. She'd stood against a wall, trying to decide how to best separate herself from a young man regaling her with a story in which he'd rescued a kitten from a tree. Excusing herself for another drink, she found the usual party fare in the kitchen. Cheap whiskey. Vodka. She opened the fridge and found orange juice and a bottle of some god-awful new energy drink. Someone had tried to spice things up with a liter of tequila housed in a terra cotta skull.

She'd been about to leave when she saw three bright cans in the fridge door, looking like the beer she usually drank but covered with a more artistic label. It showed a boy holding a loaf of bread, which wafted green steam. The whole thing was done in rubber tube style, like an old cartoon.

"You know what that is?"

Holly glanced over her shoulder. A stranger stood in the doorway, pointing to the fridge. His biceps popped from beneath white sleeves.

"Beer," Holly had said, lamely.

"Not just any beer," the man had said. "Brana Brewing's *Dough Face*. I had a friend ship six of these all the way from the Brewing Cloud. Want to try?"

One sip and Holly was hooked. Not just on the beer, but also on the man who'd shown it to her. Holly had dated Jonah for two years. When he'd scored a job on the Brewing Cloud, she'd followed him. Although the relationship hadn't survived the move, Holly had liked her new home and decided to stay. On the Cloud, the sun shone most of the year, and the air smelled like sprouting malt. The Cloud also offered the best selection of beer anywhere in the galaxy.

During her first year on the Cloud, Holly had developed a craving for juicy India Pale Ales. Then she'd switched to peppery saisons and richly layered stouts. After that, it was sours, then spontaneously fermented sours, then spontaneously fermented sours aged over vegetables. And then she was done. Hardly anything surprised her anymore.

The man next to Holly cleared his throat. He was short, the skin of his face hidden beneath a dark hood. "Bet I've heard of one place you haven't tried," he said. "Upside Down Brewing."

Holly snorted. She knew every brewery on the Cloud and Upside Down wasn't one of them.

"Oh, you scoff," the man said. "But I'm not the one complaining about a lack of innovation. Upside Down is the Cloud's greatest secret, designed to tantalize those who have tried everything. They specialize in juicy IPAs."

Her first love. With a twinge of regret, Holly thought about Jonah. About that first party, and how they'd moved to the Cloud together. About his smiling face and kind heart. About his drinking problem, and the three crazy months it took them to break up, and the strange, peculiar path he took to fame not long after.

"I'm sorry," she said, pushing back. She dropped a handful of cash on the bar. "I need to leave."

As Holly walked home, she couldn't keep her mind from wandering. *What if there is a secret brewery on the Cloud?* she thought. *Would that change anything? If I found something like that, would I stay?* Maybe it was because she missed Jonah, or because she'd had a little too much of Dr. Wunder's Renegade Whiskey at the Crow's Nest, but as soon as she got home she found herself looking for the elusive operation.

"Upside Down, Upside Down," Holly said, running her fingers down a historical index of breweries. She couldn't find it. In fact, after tearing through every book in her library, the only mention of the words "upside down" came from a popular album by the Brewing Cloud-based electronic band The Boozy Prophets, who'd produced a five song EP called "Turn Your World Upside Down." The album didn't have any lyrics; rather, the songs mostly consisted of clicks and beeps. After playing the album forward, backward, and at every possible speed, Holly conceded that it didn't contain a secret message.

That was it. She packed her bags. There were too many memories on the Cloud, and not all of them were good. She was ready to leave.

However, by pure coincidence, she set a pocket mirror atop The Boozy Prophets' album. The cover featured each of the four band members dressed in colorful pastels standing around a kick drum. And the mirror was placed just so, that when she looked into it, the strange writing on the drum actually spelled a message.

"Start in the cellars of Crystal Tree," it said. "And turn your world upside down."

No amount of cars, tourists, or natural disasters could stop Holly from getting to Crystal Tree. She reached the brewery at a run, sweat trickling down her cheeks. During regular business hours, a tour passed through Crystal Tree's cellars every thirty minutes, and she arrived just as the 3:00 PM was headed down the steps. She followed. At even intervals along the hallway sat giant foeders, huge vats made of oak planks that were used to ferment beer. She listened impatiently as the guide explained that inside each one, bacteria munched away at sugary wort, producing alcohol. As the guide led the group into the next room, Holly ducked into the shadows.

Think, she told herself. Perhaps one of the taps that stuck out of the foeders might double as a secret switch, but Holly had given enough tours at Green Smoke to know what happened when overzealous tourists touched a tap without permission. If she guessed wrong and released twenty-five barrels of beer onto the cellar floor, she'd never be allowed inside Crystal Tree again.

Come on, she thought. There were ten foeders, five along each wall. They looked the same except for the black or red bands that ran around their tops and bottoms. Was the color some type of code? Holly placed her hand on the thick wood and imagined the liquid inside. As the temperature changed, it moved in and out of the wood, picking up subtle flavors of vanilla and tobacco. Then she noticed that each container had a small red arrow below the tap. Each one pointed down, except for the arrow on Foeder #6. It pointed up.

"Could it be that easy?" she whispered.

Holly walked around Foeder #6, then dropped to her knees and peered under it. Each of the wooden vats sat on stilts, which gave them about a foot of lift. But Foeder #6 was hollow. She crawled beneath it and stood, brushing away cobwebs. On the underside of the foeder's lid was a brass plaque.

"Look down," it said.

She glanced down and saw a brass ring. Lifting it revealed a hole. A metal ladder plunged into the darkness. Holly waited until her fingers stopped trembling and then began her descent. She climbed two rungs down the ladder and pulled the trapdoor closed behind her. On its underside, she saw another plaque.

"Going Upside Down?" it said.

Holly climbed for half a minute before she saw a light below her. At first it was very small, and then she realized she was just high up. The cold of the metal rungs stung her hands and she repeated, in her head, "Upside down, upside down," over and over until it lost its meaning. Just when she thought she might lose her grip, her feet touched solid ground.

Holly caught her breath. A lantern burned beside an oak

door, twenty feet high and banded like the foeders. There was no knob, but there was a keyhole.

Holly walked over the keyhole and peered through it. Inside, she saw an opulent brewery. A dim chandelier hung from the ceiling; white napkins and silverware festooned long wooden tables. Against the back wall was a seven-barrel brewing system and stacked fifteen barrel tanks. Everything was covered in a thick layer of dust. Cobwebs made the chandelier look like cotton candy.

"Am I too late?" Holly whispered. Clearly, no one had been inside the brewery in years.

She pushed against the door but it didn't budge. She added more weight. She kicked it. Nothing happened. In exhaustion, Holly sat and put her back against the door. Even if she'd wanted, she couldn't return to the surface. She'd come so far. Could it be that her journey had ended with this locked door?

Holly squinted through the keyhole one last time, where a message seemed to materialize on the dusty backbar. "Turn around," it said.

Her eyes swept the wall behind her. In the back-left corner of the antechamber, she saw a small door, no higher than her knees.

This one had a knob, but it was also locked. A lockbox sat next to the door, but she didn't know the code. She gave a few experimental guesses. Then, screaming with frustration, she sat against the wall. What could she do? There was one option that came to her, but it wasn't pleasant. She racked her brain for another choice.

"Oh boy," she said to herself. "You're really about to do this, aren't you?"

She pulled out her cellphone. The Cloud was known for its terrific reception; even here, deep in the bowels of the space, she had service. She dialed the number she knew by heart and then deleted it. She dialed again. She took a deep breath and hit, "Call."

don'tpickupdon'tpickupdon'tpickup, she thought.

"Hello?" said a familiar voice on the other end of the line.

"Yes, hi," she said. She cleared her throat. "Hello, Jonah. It's me."

For a moment, there was silence. Holly heard the sound of splashing water. "Come back in," someone said, in the distance.

"Holly," said Mr. Smooth. "It's, uh, been a while since anyone called me that. And a while since I've heard from you. Is everything okay?"

Now it was Holly's turn to be silent. There was no malice in his voice, none of the sadness that suffused the voicemails he'd left for her in the months after their breakup. In fact, he sounded downright pleasant.

"I need your help," she said, and her voice cracked.

"Oh," he said. "This isn't the best time. I've been seeing someone—Nadia, I'll be right there—and she's great. You'd like her, Holly. You really would. And frankly, I'm really happy. I know we had something special but that was a long time ago."

Holly felt her face grow hot. "I don't want to get back together," she said, quickly. "I was hoping you could tell me about one of your friends."

Mr. Smooth laughed. For a moment, she found herself missing that high-pitched giggle. She shook it off.

"Of course," he said. "Who are you thinking about?"

"Cardinal Remus," she said. "Lead singer of The Boozy Prophets. Didn't they open for you last tour?"

"Sure," said Mr. Smooth. "Cardinal is a good friend. But he's married. Maybe you want to talk to their bassist, John Christopher? He's—"

"It's not anything like that," Holly said. "I need to know his anniversary. When is it?"

"What?"

"Just help me out."

"Oh, okay. Sure. I'll text it to you. Nadia, I'm coming. Sorry, Holly. Great to hear from you. Gotta run."

He hung up. A moment later, Holly's phone buzzed with a date. Holly stared at her phone for a second, then tried the code. The lockbox clicked open. Inside was a gold key. She placed it into the lock of the smaller door and it turned soundlessly. She stepped through.

Behind the door was a long, dark hallway. She moved inside cautiously, just in case something lay in wait. Eventually, she came to a fork in the path, and then another. At each, she ripped off a strip of cloth from her sleeve and left it at the base of the path she'd taken, just in case she needed to find her way back. Even so, after half a dozen forks, she doubted she could find her way back to the ladder. Then the walls began to close, and she knew it was hopeless. She ran, heedless of any danger, until she reached a dark pit that teamed with beer roaches. Only, these weren't the size of her palm, like the kind she occasionally found under the couches in her apartment, but the size of small dogs. They looked up at her, their antennae wiggling as they clicked their oversized mandibles.

"This is for you, Jonah," Holly said as she grabbed the rope that hung on one wall. At the sound of her voice, the roaches scattered, revealing a message on the floor beneath them.

"So you want to go Upside Down?" it said.

Holly redoubled her grip on the rope. It was thick and coarse beneath her palms. One end was attached to the ceiling above her. She gave it an experimental pull and it held. Taking a deep breath, she backed toward the door, then took a running start and threw herself across the pit.

From the end of the hallway, a jet of flame shot toward her, but she ducked into an alcove. Demons peeled off the walls and approached her, their red eyes flashing, but she stood her ground until they exposed themselves as puppets. She wanted Upside Down. She needed it and nothing could stop her.

After another hour of wandering underground, Holly came to a circular door. Above the door—written upside down, of course—were words stamped in white block letters: Upside Down Brewing.

"You can do this," Holly said, as she spun the door's handle.

Inside, steel fermentation tanks clung to the ceiling, and a fan spun on the floor. Wooden platforms hung from the ceiling on steel cables. There were tables on the platforms, not upside down, and along the back wall ran a long wooden bar.

"It's real," she whispered.

"Welcome," the bartender said, looking over his shoulder as he poured a draft. The beer arced from the upside down nozzle and he caught it in a glass. "I'm sure you're tired. Come, have a seat. First one is on the house."

He closed the tap. Holly walked to the bar and sat down.

"We have a single option," the bartender said. *"Number One.* Capital N, capital O. It makes a draught pour of Dr. Wunder's *Rarest Secret* taste like bathwater." He set the beer in front of Holly. It glowed orange and hazy beneath two inches of fluffy white head. "Cheers," said the bartender, as she took a sip. "What do you think? Turn your world upside down?"

Holly burst into tears.

Kevin Campbell's Breakfast Club

On the first Tuesday of each month, Brian Needham and Kevin Campbell ate breakfast at a diner called Kegs and Eggs. For exactly one hour, Kevin pushed eggs and sausage around his plate while Brian slurped down beer battered French toast and talked his ear off.

"I've been thinking of ways to make a little extra pocket money," Brian said, licking his fork. "You know, with little Brian's birthday coming up. I thought maybe we could host an ice cream social. All kinds of different ice cream and people would pay to eat it."

Kevin rolled his eyes. The clock above the griddle showed twenty minutes past the hour.

"This is the Brewing Cloud, not the Ice Cream Cloud," Kevin muttered, poking at his sausage. He looked at the clock again, just to double check. Still twenty minutes.

"We could have a jellybean social," Brian said, waving his fork. Syrup splattered the napkin holder. "Or just a bean social. Like a chili cook-off."

"Enough socials," Kevin said.

"Another idea," Brian said. "We could take over Dr. Wunder's Magical Medicinal Brewery and Beer Emporium."

Kevin mouthed the words as Brian said them; this was part of their routine, which Brian seemed to think was the funniest thing in the world. During every meeting, he suggested they take over operations from the Cloud's most successful brewer, and then he'd say . . .

"Just kidding. But I have another idea."

Kevin motioned for the idea with his fork.

"The other day, I was walking past Green Smoke Brewing and I saw a line out the door. It wrapped all the way down the block, past the pharmacy and the hot dog stand where the guy wears the funny wig."

"So we should take over operations from Green Smoke," Kevin said. "Great."

"No, no," said Brian, laughing. "The line wasn't for beer. It was for glasses. Beer glasses. Like, the kind you put beer into."

"Those certainly are beer glasses."

"We could make those. Everybody is doing it. Why not us?"

Kevin pushed some scrambled egg across his plate. Ninety-nine times out of a hundred, Brian was an absolute idiot. But every once in a while, he had a decent idea. People were making money on glassware—big money. When Green Smoke released a new beer, they had a line of one hundred people down the block. Each person bought a glass and a case of beer. One hundred glasses multiplied by twenty dollars per glass . . .

"Two thousand dollars," he said suddenly, startling Brian, who was halfway to shoveling another piece of French toast into his mouth. The bread slipped from the fork, landing with a plop in a pool of syrup.

"That's if we sell two hundred glasses at ten bucks each," Brian said, his round eyes wide. "You're a genius."

Kevin shook his head. "One hundred glasses at twenty bucks each," he said. He took a bite of his eggs. "We just put something on the glass that everyone likes. How about . . ."

"The Spacedogs," Brian said. "Or wait! Dr. Wunder. A Dr. Wunder glass would sell like crazy. He could be saying one of his catchphrases. 'Have you experienced Wunder?' 'A drink per day makes the doctor say yay.'"

Kevin shook his head.

"I don't want to get sued," he said. "But what about . . ."

He'd been about to take a bit of his sausage, and now he stopped, the greasy piece of meat hovering in front of his eyes. Breakfast. Breakfast was something everyone enjoyed.

"Sausage," he said. "Kevin Campbell's Breakfast Glass."

The next day, Kevin and Brian drove to the Artist's Collective Co-Working Studio, high on a hill that overlooked the Cloud. The road was long and paved with cobblestones, and Brian hit every pothole. His jalopy bucked and bounced like a wild horse. If Brian was bothered, he didn't show it, but Kevin grabbed the loose handle near his head and tried to keep down the cold spaghetti he'd eaten for breakfast.

"I was thinking," he said, once the nausea had subsided. "With Junior's birthday approaching, I thought maybe you could use some extra cash. I thought maybe I'd put up all the money for the project. And then maybe, instead of taking a percentage, I could pay you upfront. With cash."

Kevin felt the wallet through his jeans. Inside were five hundred dollars, the total amount he was prepared to give Brian.

"What are you thinking?" Brian said.

"Three hundred."

Brian's eyebrow twitched. "Are you serious?"

Kevin swallowed. He suddenly became aware of their proximity, the size of Brian's hulking hands on the car's tiny wheel.

"Uh," Kevin stammered. "I was just—"

"That's amazing of you, Kev," Brian said, reaching over and patting his leg. "One hundred percent, I'll take you up on that deal. You're a good friend."

"Well, you know me," Kevin said. He fumbled out his wallet and practically threw the bills at Brian.

The Artist's Collective Co-Working Studio was one of the Cloud's newest buildings, built of glass and steel and cantilevered over a hill that overlooked the Cloud. At its front was a plaza where young lovers gathered in the evenings; at its back, a glass wall that provided one of the best views in the city. It housed nearly all of the Cloud's great artists, as well as their students and the up-and-comers who took single offices in the building's basement, where the view was nonexistent and the rent wasn't so high.

Sam Skains was one of those basement artists. He was new to the Cloud, a transplant from London. He had terrible allergies and had left London to escape the smog. In the several months he'd been on the Cloud, his skin had cleared up, and he'd landed work with Crystal Tree Brewing, and one of the local hop farms. Nothing major, just some murals on office walls, but enough to earn his place in the Artist's Collective.

Kevin and Brian came in to find Sam seated as his desk. He was a twiggy man in his early thirties with a pair of round eyeglass frames perched on his hawkish nose. He wore a flannel shirt and a pair of tight jeans that clung to his skinny legs. His office smelled like coffee. Every conceivable surface was covered in sketches and drawings in various stages of completion.

There was only one other chair in his office, so Kevin

sat while Brian stood in the corner. Kevin explained the idea while Sam took notes on a yellow legal pad, nodding and tapping his pen against the paper.

"I love the idea," Sam said, when Kevin had finished. "I think a breakfast glass could be really successful. Maybe you could make it into some kind of club, where you meet on weekends and serve breakfast and beer. I have a couple really good friends at Crystal Tree, I'm sure they'd be into something like that. You could probably even go to a local coffee shop and collaborate with someone there. My friend Jamie works at Little Mouse Coffee."

Kevin shook his head. "We just want the glass," he said.

"Okay," Sam said. "Just the glass. A full wrap with some little dancing eggs and sausages. Maybe throw some bacon in there. Some orange juice."

"No orange juice."

"I like orange juice," said Brian.

"No orange juice."

"Sure, no orange juice. Do you have a budget? And a timeline?"

"We were hoping you could offer us a fair price," Brian said.

Sam swiveled his chair and consulted the calendar on his desk. "I could turn this around in two weeks," he said. "It'd be six hundred dollars."

Kevin snorted. "Six hundred dollars? We don't want the drawing in gold."

Sam shrugged. "That doesn't really make sense," he said. "And that's kinda what art costs. I have to do sketches, and then the drawing, and then I have to upload it and colorize everything. It'll probably take me six hours. That means

I'll be working at one hundred dollars an hour, which is way below my normal rate. I thought I'd cut you guys a break because this seems like your first project."

"First project." Kevin shook his head. He hated how shrill his voice sounded. "We can't agree to those terms. Thank you for your time, Mr. Skains."

"I actually think it's pretty fair," Brian said. He pointed at the wall, toward a glass that Sam had done for Vampire Brewing. It was a Halloween glass with different monster heads circling the glass. "Look! Your sister used him. And I like his style. The cartoons are funny."

"Goodbye, Mr. Skains," Kevin said.

Brian looked helplessly toward the artist, then shrugged and followed his brother-in-law out of the room.

That night, Kevin was lamenting over his situation at the bar when a man at the pool table next to him came over and put a hand on his shoulder. He was a balding man in dirty clothes with a beer gut to rival Kevin's own.

"Good to see you, Kevin," the man said, and it took Kevin a moment to place him. Back in high school, Kevin had been friends with a musician named Pete Groginsky. He'd been a moderately talented bassist, but Kevin remembered that he'd also dabbled in drawing. For that, he'd won an award. Or he'd talked about winning an award. Or maybe he'd talked about an award he'd hoped to win. Either way, Kevin thought this might be Pete.

"Groginsky?" he said.

"The one and only," the man said, grinning through a mouth full of broken teeth. "I couldn't help but overhearing, but it sounds like you need an artist, eh? I dabble. One hundred and fifty bucks, I'll do anything you want."

Kevin smiled and held out his hand.

"You've got yourself a deal," he said.

For two weeks, Kevin couldn't stop thinking about the glass. He thought about it during work. He sketched it on the back of cocktail napkins. It showed up in his dreams. If his idea worked, he could buy his own car, and then he wouldn't need Brian. And if he ran the idea again, and printed a second glass, and then a third, he could probably quit his job. Maybe he'd move to Earth, to someplace sunny like New Orleans or Key West. Maybe he'd take up a hobby, like fishing. Maybe he'd buy a boat. For the first time in his life, things were looking up.

On the appointed day, Kevin got into Brian's jalopy and they drove toward the farms, where Pete Groginsky lived in a trailer. Kevin didn't particularly care for the shabby dwelling, but he consoled himself with the fact that the project was almost complete.

Groginsky met them in the yard. Just like the last time Kevin had seen him, he wore dirty clothes, and his thin wisps of gray hair were plastered to his greasy pate. An unidentifiable brown stain was smeared across the front of his shirt.

"I got what you wanted," Pete said, holding up a folded piece of paper. His nails were chipped and black, like he'd been scratching in the dirt. "You got the money?"

Kevin handed him an envelope. Pete handed him the paper.

"Pleasure doing business with you," he said, as Kevin unfolded it. He turned to leave.

"What . . . what is this?" Kevin said.

The artist turned and smiled proudly. "Your sausage,"

he said.

"Looks more like a peanut," Brian said.

"It's a potato?" said Kevin. "Not even."

Pete's face turned dark. Kevin suddenly remembered a rumor he'd heard back in high school, that Pete had broken a man's arm for laughing at his music. How had he forgotten that?

"You making fun of my art?" Pete said, quietly.

"Not at all," Kevin said.

"Well good," Pete said, turning back toward the trailer. "Like I said, Campbell, a pleasure doing business. Definitely don't hesitate to call."

In the end, Kevin and Brian went back to Sam. But with the disaster that was Pete Groginsky's drawing, they were $750 in the hole already. Then there was the $300 Kevin had paid to buy the project from Brian, which left him with a debt of $1,050 dollars. Kevin was watching his profits shrink before his eyes.

"Unbelievable," he grumbled, as he dialed an Earth-based number for a glass printer. He would've preferred to use someone on the Cloud, to cut down on shipping costs, but only one supplier printed on the type of glass he wanted, and that came from somewhere called Kansas.

"Hello and thanks for calling Gymnasium, home of full color organic printing on the Rounded Bowl 3.0, the most popular beer glass in the galaxy," said the woman who answered the phone. "This is Marsha, how can I help you?"

Kevin told her what he needed.

"Great," Marsha said. "Sounds fantastic. Just so you know, the wait time on the Rounded Bowl 3.0 is three months."

"Three months?" Kevin was incredulous. "I only want a hundred of them."

"In that case, it's four months. We have to prioritize larger orders. Though, there's a chance we get another printer soon. Obviously no guarantees, because it's coming from Germany, but that'll cut down your wait time to three and a half months. If we get the printer."

"Three and a half months. And what's the cost per item?"

"For a hundred glasses? Eight dollars and thirty nine cents. That's before shipping and tax."

Upon its release, Kevin Campbell's Breakfast Glass was a runaway success. He sold every one and even got written up by the local paper. At a cost of $19.65 per glass, Kevin walked away with $35.

"What a thrill," Brian said, taking a long sip of orange juice from the Breakfast glass. As a show of support for two of their regular customers, Kegs and Eggs had bought two of the glasses, which they kept behind the register and pulled out whenever Kevin and Brian took their regular seats. "Three hundred bucks. And I get to drink out of my own glass." Brian picked up his fork and knife. "Say, I've got another idea. Why don't we take over Dr. Wunder's Magical Medicinal Brewery and Beer Emporium?"

Kevin sighed and took a bite of his eggs.

Queen of Green

Vanilla. Nutmeg. Bergamot spice.

The bookish, brilliant, and completely blind Dr. Harold Crumb set down the tapered glass on the table in front of him and made a few notes on his clipboard. The glass rested with scarcely an inch on either side, so covered was the table in samples, each in an identical glass covered by an unblemished coaster.

Dr. Crumb brought another glass to his nose. Lemongrass. Pepper. Barnyard funk. He took another sniff. Pear. Coriander. And . . . what was that last ingredient? Dr. Crumb shook his head. This was impossible. He tried again. Now there was honey. A little citrus. And . . .

He couldn't quite place it.

For thirty-seven years, Dr. Crumb had worked as a sensory analyst, picking up aromas and tertiary flavors too delicate for machinery. In all that time, he'd never missed his mark. Sure, there had been some close calls, especially around Gustav Wunder's beers. But at the end of the day, Dr. Crumb nailed the profile every time.

"Early bird gets the worm, eh Dr. Crumb?" said Elizabeth Beck, founder of Green Smoke Brewing. It was 8:32 AM and she always called as early as possible. "Or should I say, early farmer gets the hop. I should really create some more appropriate aphorisms."

"Morning, Liza," said Dr. Crumb, cradling the phone to his ear. "I've been running sensory on the three products you sent. I have good news. No butyric acid in the Green Goddess Gose. Tart. Crisp. Lime peel. Black limes. A pinch of salt. I think it'd go excellent with trout."

"As was intended. I trust the others were technically sound?"

Dr. Crumb nodded. "You've always watched your pH and temperature. No tetrahydropyridine in the Great Green Berliner Weisse. Blackberry. Lime again. I commend your restraint with the lactose. An impeccable product, really well done."

Liza slurped her tea. "Yes, well, we had some extra product from the Gose. Thought limes could punch up the Berliner. And you know I've always gone easy on milk sugars."

"One of the many qualities for which you have my admiration. And that, ah, brings me to the final beer you sent. Queen of Green Saison. A perfect example of the style. The coriander is magical. And yet . . . there was one ingredient I couldn't quite place. Something . . . well, if I knew what it was, I'd be able to tell you. But my sense was, you used something special in this beer. Something unusual. Do you know what I'm talking about?"

There was silence on the other line. Then, "I know exactly what you're talking about."

Dr. Crumb sat back in his chair. Even if he didn't know the specific ingredient, it was reassuring to hear he hadn't lost his touch.

"And what was it?"

Silence again. Then, "For that, Dr. Crumb, you'll need to hear a story."

Elizabeth Becker's office was hung with ornaments from travels all over the world. There was a bookshelf painted red—he'd had to ask her to confirm the color, but after feeling the other items in the room, he'd already known. One shelf held rocks, dried roots, and a double barreled wooden flute. Another was filled with candles of varying sizes, the wax dripping to form stalactites that framed in the books on the shelf below. The whole room smelled like . . . ah. She was burning palo santo.

"Doctor, take a seat, please," said Liza, as one of her taproom managers escorted him into the room. She didn't condescend him by pulling out a chair; he felt his way to the leather seat and sat down. "Can I get you something to drink? Water? Beer? Tea?"

Dr. Crumb could smell her cinnamon cardamom chai. He waved dismissively. "I must admit, I'm more interested in this mysterious ingredient and story," he said. "Something that couldn't be shared over the phone."

Liza sipped her tea. "I could've shared it over the phone," she said. "But I think the story will have more gravity in person. Stories have power, Dr. Crumb. You of all people should know that."

Again, Dr. Crumb waved. "Go on then. Let's hear it."

Liza's chair creaked. "How much do you know of my story before I came to the Cloud?"

Dr. Crumb shrugged. He didn't know much, just that she'd been in Peru. As to what had brought her to the Cloud, he couldn't say, though he'd heard rumors: running from a man, running to a man, a promise to a dying grandmother.

"Not much," he admitted. "I know you spent time in Peru."

"Yes. I was born in San Francisco, but this story starts in Lima. That's where I went after a terrible breakup. I'd heard about a retreat in the Amazon that could only be reached by boat. There was no noise, no distractions. You were just as likely to see an emerald tree boa as you were to hear news from the outside. As someone looking for a fresh start, it was an ideal situation. So I went down to Peru with a backpack and a yearning for something new. Although I didn't speak Spanish, I found someone who knew exactly what I was talking about. He was a translator for a tour company. He took me to his friend, a boat driver, and told him what I needed. In hindsight, it was a strange situation, but it was also a strange time in my life. I was open to anything and I really didn't care what happened to me. I paid the driver, got into his boat, and we headed up the river. My driver pointed out a cayman, which is something like a crocodile, and a three-toed sloth. When a tarantula fell into the boat, he calmly scooped it out and set it on a tree branch."

Dr. Crumb shivered. "I hate spiders," he said.

Liza laughed. "There's certainly no shortage of them in the Amazon. Big ones. Hairy. Luckily, they're pretty docile, unless you're prey. I saw half a dozen as we moved toward our destination: The Lodge. That's what my translator had called it, and that's the only English word the driver spoke. 'Lodge,' he called. 'Lodge, Lodge.' It sat on stilts in the middle of the river, its roof covered in thatch. The driver threw my bags on the dock and yelled at me in Spanish, and then he drove away."

"And you weren't worried?"

He heard the soft rustle of clothing as Liza shrugged. "I wasn't thinking about that. I knew I needed to get away. And the remoteness of the place, the strangeness of it all, felt right. I wasn't scared. I was excited. Anyways, when no one came to greet me, I gathered my bags and headed into the first building I saw. There were about twenty people at low tables, eating bowls of black beans and fish. I'd arrived during dinner. No one looked up. I waited around for a while, to see if anyone would talk to me, and then continued to explore. I found a couple rooms, which had bags in them, and then an empty one, which I claimed. It had a low bed with a thin mattress and a small night table. The bed was covered in mosquito netting. You could see right out into the jungle. Bathrooms were communal, and in addition to the dining room, there was a room for meditation, covered in woven mats."

"That was it?"

"That's it. I was invisible and I loved it. I'd rise with the sun, or when a caiman slapped its tail against one of the wooden poles that held up my room, and walk into the main room for a piece of fruit. Then I'd just . . . sit. And think. Then lunch, which was usually roasted root vegetables, and more thinking, and dinner. In those early days, I had a lot of thoughts. Mostly about my ex, but after a while, there was no new territory to cover. I let it go. Then my thoughts turned to my young adulthood, and how I'd come to be in a silent retreat in the middle of the rainforest. That led to my childhood, but eventually there was nothing new left there, either."

"How much time passed?" Dr. Crumb asked.

"Four months."

"Without a word?"

"Nada. I don't think I could do it again, but like I said, at the time, it was just what I needed. Four months, and I'd thought through my past from every angle. My life had been perfectly reconciled. That's when I began to think about the future. You'd think, with any option open to me, that I'd face a paradox of choice. That with so many options, it'd be impossible to choose one. But without a hundred voices in my ear, the advice and thoughts, experiences and fears of everyone I'd ever met, it was actually quite easy. I made a choice. I decided to head up to the Cloud, which was just becoming popular, and see what I could make of myself. And if it didn't work out, I could always change direction. To answer your earlier question, people came to the Lodge periodically. Not often, but every once in a while. You could hear the put-put-put of the motor from a couple hundred yards away. If you wanted to leave, you'd have your bags packed. When the boat came, you'd throw them in and head back with the driver. And worst case scenario, a man named Claudio dropped off food every two weeks, so you could always go back with him."

"You packed your bags," said Dr. Crumb.

"No one had seen me pack, but everyone knew I was leaving," said Liza. "For the first time, I got the occasional nod from the other people at the Lodge, especially the ones that had been there the longest. The day before I left for good, I was approached by the man who ran the Lodge, an aging shaman who always wore a red scarf. Without saying anything, I knew I was supposed to follow him. He led me down to the dock and into the small wooden rowboat he sometimes used to head into the jungle and collect ingredients that would supplement our meals. I took a seat in the rickety craft and the shaman handed me a lantern. Then he picked up the oars and began to row. I had no idea where we were going. I'd say he rowed for about an hour before we entered a tunnel made from tree branches that overhung the river. The light was going down, but I could see speckles of sky between the branches. Then, nothing. The vines and leaves and branches formed a ceiling too thick for light to penetrate. The shaman rowed for a while longer before I felt something scrape along the bottom of the boat. When he lit the lantern, I saw we were on a beach of sorts, covered in caiman. Albino caiman. There were fifteen of them, maybe twenty. I could see their translucent skin and red eyes. Between them, a path ran to a wooden door. The shaman got out of the boat and motioned me to follow. I wasn't going to get out but he laughed and skipped down the path. The caimans didn't move. And he had the lantern, so it was either sit in the dark or follow him down the path. So I followed. When we reached the door, he handed me the lantern and motioned me inside. Then he closed the door behind me. I heard him drop the latch.

"'Hey,' I said. It was the first word I'd spoken in months. Can you imagine? Four months of silence, and my first word was 'Hey.' But it's also not every day that a silent shaman brings you into a tunnel in the Amazon and closes you into a circular room. Because that's where I was—a perfectly round room. It was maybe ten yards in diameter. The walls were made of damp earth that glistened in the lamplight. In the middle of the room was a stone basin and on the far side was another door. I tried both doors but they were locked.

So I went to the basin. It was filled with water. It was clearly ceremonial, so I dipped my fingers into it, just deep enough to break the surface. It was cold. After being in the Amazon for four months, it was strange to feel something cool, especially water. It smelled faintly of orchids. I splashed a bit across my face and tried the doors again. Still locked. There were no other exits to the room."

Dr. Crumb felt his pulse quicken. "So what did you do?"

"I sat. And sat. Hours passed, I think. Eventually, I got thirsty, so I drank that water. That was a mistake. There was something in that basin, something that made my temples pound and the walls breathe. I thought I'd left my life behind, but it wasn't until I'd consumed that water that I finally, truly committed to a new path. When I regained some semblance of normal consciousness, the far door was open, and the basin was empty of liquid. At its bottom was a strange ingredient, which I knew I'd put into a beer."

Dr. Crumb leaned forward. "This ingredient," he said. "This was the one in your saison?"

"Yes. I walked through the open door and found myself at the Lodge. There was a boat at the docks. My bags were already inside. I hopped a ride, got back to Lima, and booked immediate travel to the Brewing Cloud."

Dr. Crumb laughed. "But what was it?" he said. "What was the ingredient?"

Liza shrugged. "You're a blind sensory analyst with a thirty-seven year flawless record," she said. "I won't ruin your story."

Back in his workshop, Dr. Crumb reflected on Queen of Green. Could it be that the secret ingredient was something native to the Amazon? Perhaps. He went to his fridge and poured off another sample. Coriander, of course. Pear . . .

There it was. The secret ingredient. He ran through his exhaustive list of South American flavors, but nothing fit the bill. Cassava? No. He couldn't see that being very good in a beer. But what was it?

Dr. Crumb sat back and breathed slowly. He'd never been stumped before. It was a testament to Liza Becker's skill that three weeks later, he was still thinking about the mysterious liquid, the flavor profiles rolling around between his ears with the details of her strange story.

"That's it!" he said, smiling. "Carrots."

And he was right.

The Notes of
Mr. Henry Wunder

Dictated by Henry Wunder

Recorded and Prepared by Alistair Gray

Alligator Brewing, The Cloud || Oxfordshire, England

Alistair Gray: Are you ready?

Henry Wunder: Just a minute. Ah, that's better. Thing keeps poking me.

AG: No worries. I have to admit, I'm glad you agreed to speak with me. My research hit a bit of a wall on the Cloud. I thought I was at a dead end until I found your lineage.

HW: Ah yes, Wunder isn't a particularly common last name. To my knowledge, it's just me and my sister now.

AG: And Gustav? And his daughter?

HW: Yes, you'd mentioned them in your email. That's why I'm a little confused. That's why I wanted to talk.

AG: Excellent. And you're aware you're being recorded?

HW: Yes.

AG: Okay then. Tell me what you know about Gustav.

HW: Well, let's see. As children, my sister Maude and I visited our Uncle Emmerick Wunder's country mansion. He'd had been married, then; it wasn't until a few years later my Aunt Millie died. And they had a son, Gustav. All I remember about her was that her hair looked like a bird's nest and she smelled like boiled peanuts. I have that strong impression: boiled peanuts. She liked to dress up in lace, like she was going to a ball, but she never left the house. As for their son, I'd never met him. Even as a child, I found it strange I'd never met my cousin, but my uncle was a strange man. I remember one night, in front of a roaring fireplace, when he'd told us of the night he'd spent curled up in a moth-ridden sleeping bag on the floor of the family mausoleum, searching for evidence of the afterlife.

"Like ghosts?" I'd asked. "Are they real?"

His dark brown eyes had blazed in the light. "Oh, very real," he said. "Very, very real."

That's the kind of thing you remember as a child. But throughout our childhoods and well into adulthood, Uncle Emmerick and his eccentricities existed only as distant specters. We didn't think of him much until we each got a letter, some thirty years later, inviting us back to visit. I think Maude and I both surprised each other by accepting. But an isolated country retreat sounded like just the ticket, and I did want to meet Gustav. I didn't even know what he looked like! Even my mother had never met her nephew. I have to admit, I was a bit worried that we'd spend the week wiping drool from our old uncle's chin, but when the hired car that picked us up from the train station pulled up to Uncle Emmerick's mansion, he wasn't at all like I expected.

AG: How's that?

HW: Well, I expected him to be old. Senile. But he was entirely lucid, entirely pleasant. The second we stepped from the car, he bent and stared into Maude's eyes. "Ah," he said. "Just like Melissa's. And you," he looked at me, "your mother's smile. I was so sorry to hear about her passing."

Of course, my mother had died a decade earlier, but I didn't say anything. Honestly, I couldn't get over how good he looked. Trim waist, bright eyes, glowing skin. He must have been seventy but looked ten years younger. He tried to take my briefcase but I insisted on carrying it myself. But really, it looked like he could've taken Maude's and mine and run two miles.

He gave us a tour. The outside of the house sparkled, but the inside was old and somewhat sad. Much of the furniture had been covered with white cloth, and the tour was confusing, far more twisted than I remembered from my youth. Several hallways seemed to lead to nowhere and stairs that should've gone to the attic stopped halfway to the ceiling. I got turned around several times but Uncle Emmerick always pointed out the way with a chuckle and a clap of his hands, as if he found my confusion delightful. At some point, we came to a door where someone had painted "Keep Out" in black letters across the upper third. That struck me as odd, until my uncle said, "This is Gustav's room." He knocked but no one replied. "Gustav?" he said. When no one answered, he said, more loudly, "Your cousins are here. They've come all the way from the city." Still, there was no response. "A shy boy," he said, and then leaned in and confided, as if it were a secret, "He doesn't like strangers."

After that, Uncle Emmerick left us to our own devices. You'd think that, after his pleading letter, he'd want to spend time with us, but no. He sat in his study and smoked his pipe while Maude and I walked around. In one alcove, I saw an urn that supposedly contained the ashes of Akhenaten, the heretic pharaoh, father of King Tut. I've since donated them to the British Museum. And I walked the grounds, which ran for miles. Maude spent most of her time in the solarium, writing notes in the margins of whatever book she was reading.

On our third day I went to join her, but she wasn't there. So I sat and read a book that I'd found on the nightstand of my quarters: it was bound in the softest red leather, stamped with gold typography. Really, it felt like human skin. The book was called *Gehenna*, and it was written by my uncle. I think this might be the only copy that exists. May I read you the prologue? Here we are. 'In nineteen thirty five, Erwin Schrödinger came up with a famous thought experiment to demonstrate the quantum theory of superposition, which states that the act of observing something causes it to exist. To demonstrate his theory, Schrödinger talked about placing a cat in a steel box with a flask of poison, a Geiger counter, and a bit of radioactive material so small that, over the course of an hour, there was a fifty percent chance that the Geiger counter would pick up some radiation, and a fifty percent chance that it wouldn't. In the event that the counter detected radiation, the flask would shatter and the poison would kill the cat. Otherwise, the cat survived.'"

AG: That's the famous Schrödinger's Cat Experiment.

HW: Exactly. But my uncle adds his own commentary. 'There are two leading interpretations for this experiment,' he writes. 'The first says that until the box is opened, the cat is fifty percent alive and fifty percent dead. It's the act of observation, or opening the box, that forces the cat to take one of the states, but until that happens the cat actually exists in a blurred state of both life and death to those outside the box. This is called the Copenhagen Interpretation. The second interpretation says that opening the box creates two different realities: one where the cat is dead, and another where the cat is alive. This is called the Many-Worlds Interpretation.

'In this book I present a third state, a state guaranteed to shatter convention and shake our conception of post-humous reality. With irrevocable proof, I shall demonstrate that the simple act of observing the experiment causes the cat to live, either in life or life after death; it is only when the cat is placed in the box and forgotten, alienated from any who might observe its passing, that the cat becomes doomed. For to make the transition without being observed—or, at the least, remembered—is to enter the heinous, horrifying, otherworldly realm of Gehenna.'

AG: That's quite the opening.

HW: Isn't it? My uncle was crazy. Completely insane. The rest of the book is filled with mathematical proofs, graphs, incantations, and symbols. Chapter three details the creation of a very complex brew that supposedly grants visions of the future. The liquid needs chants, star alignment, bezoar stones, that sort of thing. Chapter six is about reaching other dimensions. Chapter eight is about extending your life and even bringing yourself back to life. If he'd published the thing as fiction, he would've have made a million pounds! I've half a mind to publish it myself.

AG: And how does this relate to Gustav?

HW: Well, I'm getting there. Chapter four contains clips of messages that my uncle had supposedly retrieved from Gehenna. He actually claimed to have gone there. Let's see if I can find a few, just so you get a sense . . . Ah! Yes: 'Why did I kill her? I sinned and now I suffer for it. She laughs! She laughs!' Or, here's another: 'Hell. This is hell for sure. Why can't I die?' And here's a cheerful treasure: 'Beloved, beloved, come to me! Come to me, beloved!' There's a note here that explains this last phrase was repeated four hundred and forty-four times. The voice remained silent for four minutes and forty-four seconds before repeating the phrase four hundred and forty-four more times.

AG: Horrifying.

HW: Certainly. Personally, I'm not just horrified that he heard these things, or thought he heard these things, but that he sat there and listened to someone saying, "Beloved,

beloved, come to me," four hundred and forty-four times, and then waited through four minutes of silence before listening to it again! Just . . . insane!

AG: Evidently.

HW: Anyways, this is what I was reading when Maude walked into the room and announced that Uncle Emmerick had shot himself.

AG: What?

HW: That's what I said. "What?" And Maude told me again that he'd shot himself in the head.

AG: What?

HW: Yes. So we both acknowledged that we should call the police, but neither of us made a move toward the kitchen. Instead, we walked down a long corridor, through the mansion's ornate entry to the west wing, where my uncle kept his private study. I remember that Maude paused at the door.
    "You don't get scared from blood, do you?" she asked.
    "No," I said, which wasn't true. I'm terrified of blood. But I wanted to see what had happened. So Maude pushed open the door. And true enough, Uncle Emmerick had shot himself. He sat slumped in a black leather chair, right here, right where I'm sitting now. His arms dangled and blood and bits of brain and bone sullied the ancient books on the wall behind him. On the floor beside him lay a snub-nosed grey revolver with a wooden stock, and on the desk in front

of him, right where I'm sitting, was a note. "I'm following the instructions detailed in Chapter Eight of *Gehenna*," it said. "Wish me luck." If you remember, Chapter Eight was about coming back from the dead. But clearly, something had gone wrong because the man was dead. And as I stood there, watching his blood dribble along the floor, it occurred to me that someone should tell our cousin.

AG: Gustav.

HW: I told you I was getting there. Maude generously suggested I be the one to tell him.

"Call the police," I said. "I'll meet you in the kitchen."

So I walked to the foyer and began climbing one of those sweeping staircases. I got halfway down a corridor before realizing I was walking in the wrong direction. I found the right way, but I have to tell you, that was the scariest five minutes of my life. This place can be disorienting, when you don't know it, and every time I turned a corner I thought I'd run into my uncle's mangled corpse. But finally I found my way back to the place where I'd gotten lost and soon recognized the paint on Gustav's door.

"Gustav?" I said, knocking. No answer. "Gus," I said, knocking again with more force. Still, there was no answer. "Gustav, I need to speak with you." I realized that the boy might be scared of a stranger, so I quickly added, "It's your cousin, Henry."

AG: Did he come?

HW: What do you think?

AG: No.

HW: Of course not. I tried the door, but it was locked. I went back down the hall, to try and find Maude, but got lost again. For one brief, crushing moment I thought I was alone. Then I heard Maude's voice drifting through one of the corridors: "Henry, this way!" I've never been so glad to hear another voice in my life. We spent the next half hour trying to convince Gustav to come out. But he wouldn't come. When the police arrived, he still hadn't come, and one of the officers suggested we break down the door. We stood to one side as he rolled up his sleeves. On the fourth kick, the door finally broke.

"Gustav," the officer said, stepping into the room. And you know what we saw?

AG: I have no idea.

HW: We saw nothing. He didn't exist.

AG: What do you mean?

HW: The room didn't have any windows. There was nothing in it. No bed, no furniture, no doors save the one. There was dust everywhere. It wasn't disturbed by anyone except me and the officer. No one had been inside the room. Gustav didn't exist.

AG: Then . . . ?

HW: That's the question I asked myself. Why the charade?

AG: That's right!

HW: To be honest, I don't really know. But I have a hypothesis. I did some digging and you know what I found? Aunt Millie wasn't the only one who'd died in childbirth. Her unborn son Gustav had died as well.

AG: I still don't—?

HW: Here's the genius of it, and you have to read this book to understand. My uncle was a single bachelor living by himself. His magnum-opus was a book called *Gehenna,* in part about a hellacious, solitary realm where you go if you die without anyone remembering you. He believed in it. See? He believed this place existed, that he'd received messages from it. And he wanted to try his whole coming back from the dead thing, but he was scared for Gustav, that no one would remember Gustav if something went wrong and he wasn't around. And he was scared for himself. If he made a mistake, and no one remembered him, he'd also be confined to that place.

AG: So he pretended that Gustav had never died.

HW: Exactly. And what about him? Who would remember him if he died? Why, his dear old niece and nephew. Because how could anyone forget the time that their uncle invited them on holiday and blew his brains out instead?

AG: I imagine that'd be difficult.

HW: Quite.

AG: But . . . if he's dead, then . . . who is Gustav Wunder?

HW: The only Gustav Wunder I know has been dead some fifty years, and that's only if you count an unborn fetus as alive to begin with. That's why I was so confused when you mentioned some of his recent work. It sounds like you've got quite a mystery on your hands.

Dr. Wunder's Magical Medicinal Brewery and Beer Emporium

I was sitting in the corner when Bill Campbell came in and said, "Hey Z, you hear about the contest?"

Bill was always talking and I wasn't in a mood to pay him mind. "I don't know what you're talking about," I said, biting into my bologna.

"Of course you don't," Bill said. "Always sitting down here by your lonesome. Ain't right for a young lady." He cleared a space for his lunch pail and sat down. "You should be out and about. When I was sixteen, I . . ."

I tuned Bill out. He always had something to say—usually it was about one get-rich-quick scheme or another. His family was the same way. I knew he had a daughter who'd sold her brewery to Champagne Equities, and everyone knew their reputation. And about a month before, Bill's son Kevin had been arrested for peddling counterfeit glassware. Probably Bill insisted on talking to me because I was all he had left.

However, I perked up when Bill said, "Dr. Wunder is giving away five recipes to people who find secret codes on his labels. And he's not giving away regular recipes, either. Think Rare Recipes." Bill paused because he knew he had my attention. "But you wouldn't know about that," he said.

"Because you're down here."

Now I noticed the roar from upstairs. Sometimes I got so focused on my work I lost everything around me. Bill would tell me stories all day, and by night I couldn't remember a word he'd said.

"Go on," Bill said. "You go upstairs and see if I'm lying."

It was a long way to the tap room, up past the barrel room, the hop processing room, the malting room, the lab, the granary, and cold storage. The whole way up, my heart was pounding, and not just because of the climb. Dr. Wunder's beer was the most secretive brewery on the Cloud. They didn't open their brewery to anyone. They only distributed to other breweries, bars, and bottle shops around the Cloud, and their rare bottle releases happened at random locations. You could see the smokestacks of their brewery peeking above high stone walls, and tourists loved taking pictures of the front iron gate, but no one ever got inside. And no one ever came out. Vans pulled up to the gates, and drivers would roll empty kegs and supplies through chutes in the wall. But the gate? Locked as long as anyone could remember.

Dr. Wunder's bottled eight staples, plus five seasonal releases that drew people from all across the earth and sky. The staples, like *Crunchbar* and *Bubblegum Blast,* weren't so hard to find, but the seasonal releases were a different story. And The Rare Recipes? People called them "rare" for a reason. You always knew when there was a rare release because the population of the Cloud doubled. If you got yourself a bottle, you could eat for half a year. If you could be the one making the recipe, instead of selling a single bottle . . . one of the Rare Release recipes could earn millions, if not hundreds of millions. I didn't have the money to spend on beer, but for a moment, I let myself dream: if I had that recipe, I'd never have to worry again.

I reached the taproom and pushed open the door. The room was filled to bursting. People lined up at the bar, waving money and shouting at the bartenders. Even Ms. Alma was behind the bar—she must've come down from her office to help. The bartenders were pulling beers out of the fridge as fast as they could, cracking off the caps and pressing bottles directly into waving hands. Only, people weren't buying Alligator Brewing beers. The brown bottles boasted bright purple and green labels and gold caps. It was all Dr. Wunder product.

Now, I loved Alligator Brewing—worked there with Daddy since I could walk, and Ms. Alma kept food in my fridge—but Dr. Wunder beer was something else. If he was giving away a Rare Recipe to the person who found a secret code beneath the label of one of his beers, it was no surprise the taproom was such a madhouse.

"Give me another one!" a man in an orange coat shouted, and a bartender took his money and slapped a beer into his hand. Without even taking a sip, the man peeled off the label and checked the back. Disgusted, he set the untouched beer on the bar and pushed against the crowd. The counter was filled with full beers: Dr. Wunder's *Crunchbar, Bubblegum Blast, Extra Berry Chocolate Tummy Tickler.*

"Let me up, I was here before any of you," shouted a woman with long brown hair, clawing at the shoulder of the man in front of her. Then she disappeared beneath the sea of bodies. It was chaos. I'd never seen Alligator so busy on a Tuesday.

That evening, Ms. Alma called the whole Alligator team

into her office. The bar staff had brought chairs in from the brewery, though it was still standing room only. I crouched beside Ms. Alma's bookshelf, the smallest space allocated for the team's smallest member. When everyone was inside and the door was closed, Ms. Alma began.

"You've probably heard the news," she said. "I've been in touch with a representative from the Wunder Brewery and the rumors are true."

A gasp swept the room. People immediately began talking amongst themselves.

"For those of you who have been living under a rock," Ms. Alma said, over the noise, "Dr. Wunder has hidden five secret codes behind five of his labels. The codes could be on any one of his brands, at any bar, brewery, or bottle shop across the Cloud. If you find one of the codes, you get to choose one of Dr. Wunder's Rare Recipes."

Another ripple of conversation ran across the room and Ms. Alma banged on her desk.

"Enough," she said. "This doesn't change much. We're still in the business of providing beer to thirsty customers. Just be prepared to serve a little more Wunder beer than Alligator for a while. I'm going to have a separate meeting with the production team to see if we can get some more lager in the tanks, or if we might be able to lay some stout in barrels. Look at this as the opportunity to experiment with some of the longer timeline beers we've been talking about." She cast a sharp glare around the room. "And if I hear you're responsible for a single Wunder beer missing from inventory, you're fired. No exceptions."

After opening the floor, Ms. Alma dismissed us. Although she'd answered a good many of our questions, the big one was still on everyone's lips: When would the first code get found? As it turned out, we didn't have to wait long for an answer. That very evening, the first code was discovered by a lucky local named Anne Westing. I knew her from a dive bar called the Crow's Nest. She was a regular. Tall blonde woman, liked to wear overalls and work boots. She worked a hop farm on the far eastern end of the Cloud and was always friendly, and I was glad a local found the first code. I'm surprised she even made it to the bar, on account of all the tourists. Ever since the announcement, they'd been arriving by the boatful. Hardly a minute went by without a new transport vessel pulling up to the docks. Alligator swam with them—Ms. Alma called in all the staff on overtime. Even Bill and I took shifts behind the bar. You couldn't walk half a block without some drunk tourist stumbling over your shoes.

The best part of Anne finding the code? She wasn't even trying. Rather, she was going about her nightly ritual of drinking at the Crow's Nest after work. I guess the owner of the bar roped off a small section for VIPs, but really it was just for his regular customers. The Crow's Nest was a second home for a lot of us. Anne was just shooting the old by and by when Corey slid her a *Crunchbar*. She popped the cap and a geyser of gold liquid shot five feet into the air. Didn't even need to check the label to know she'd won. Corey wasn't even mad at the mess—I saw him on the news, looking like the father of a beautiful newborn.

"We offer the largest selection of rare beers on the Cloud," he said, beaming at the reporter. He had a towel slung over one shoulder. For once in his life, he wore a clean shirt. "Today, we stood by that motto."

They also interviewed Anne: "City folk think living on the Cloud is a walk through a hop farm, but it's the hardest thing going," she said, tugging at one of her blonde braids. She flexed her left arm, and her bicep popped a few inches. "When I get that recipe, I'm going to start my own brewery, and I'm only going to hire kids trying to escape life on the hop farm. That's a promise."

You think people would've been discouraged, but they only doubled down. Everyone wanted a winning beer. I saw the offers—a million dollars, two million, ten million. A man from Mars offered Anne a mansion, as well as a full-time staff paid ten years in advance. Some enterprising woman put up a forty-one foot yacht, and a Plutonian Mastiff, green as the planet itself. Anne turned it all down. You couldn't put a price on a Rare Recipe. Anyways, she was a hop farmer. What was she going to do with a yacht?

That was the end of the VIP section at the Crow's Nest. There was a line outside that ran three hundred yards down the block. Corey needed all the space he could get. Still, no one blamed him. He took care of locals and we were happy for him.

But the next code wasn't found at the Crow's Nest, but somewhere a little closer to home. The next morning, Bill and I heard a roar from upstairs. "Go on," Bill said, pointing to the door with his wrench. With his other hand, he banged on his stiff left leg. "You shouldn't miss this and your shift is practically over. Go see history in the making."

I left him with the boiler and ran upstairs. Once I reached the taproom, I almost needed to cover my ears. In the middle of the room, up on the shoulders of a few men, was a boy who couldn't have been that much older than myself. He wasn't from the Cloud—I knew that instantly. He was too clean, too good looking. His clothes were too fine. And he kept hoisting his winning bottle into the air and whooping, like he'd just won some grand race.

The lucky fool. I couldn't stand to look at him for long and went back downstairs, where Bill had his head stuck in one of the boiler's trickier gearboxes.

"What are you doing back?" he said, looking up as I came into the room. "You were supposed to celebrate. Have a drink."

"I—"

"You don't got no money," Bill said. He slapped a palm against his grease-stained forehead. "I should've thought of that. I know you've been living hard since your daddy died." He dug into his pocket and removed a roll of bills. "Take—"

"I'm fine, Bill," I said. "I have my own money."

It wasn't true. I cooked all my dinners on a tiny camping stove, and earlier that week it'd finally conked out. Also, squirrels had gotten into my walls and some neighborhood kid had broken my front window.

Somehow, Bill knew. "Go on," he said, waving the bills. But instead of taking the money, I walked out of the room.

"Wowee," whistled Bill, as I left. "Ain't never seen a girl so sad to buy herself a drink."

I walked home in a daze. For some reason, I couldn't get that winning boy's face out of my head. Later, I saw him on the news. His name was Eric Darwin from Earth. In the frame behind him stood a bunch of other boys with bulging muscles, clean faces, and clothes all finery.

"Me and the boys were cruising around for Spring Break when we heard," he said. "We were supposed to go to Miami because Jason has a mansion there—shoutout Jason!—but instead we came straight here. I think we must've had two hundred beers between us. I knew we'd find a winning bottle."

"Number one," one of his friends shouted, holding up his index finger.

"And what do you plan to do with your recipe?" the reporter asked.

"Oh, I don't know," Eric said, scratching his square chin. "I want to see how it plays out. I mean, this is a once in a lifetime opportunity. Got to take advantage of life, right? Carpe diem and all that?"

"Number one!" his friend shouted, again.

I couldn't take it. What did privileged folks understand about beer? I felt relieved to be home, away from the crowds of Brewery Row. In the few blocks from Alligator to Crystal Tree, I saw four different people vomit.

Still, the fact that I was glad to be home said a lot. I occupied a single room which held a fridge, a chest of drawers, and a creaky futon. When Daddy died, he left me a couple of gold coins, but I'd long since sold those to pay my rent. I was barely getting by. I had to deal with a broken stove, a cracked window, and beer roaches. I hated those bugs. They grew twice the size of normal roaches, and their antennae stretched four or five times the length of their bodies. When mad, they hissed something fierce and beat their papery wings. They infested the eastern part of the Cloud where I lived, and you could never put down enough glue traps to make any significant dent in their numbers.

I turned off the TV and walked into the bedroom. The door creaked when I pushed it open. Almost immediately, I heard a rustling sound, like someone flipping through one of the big books in Ms. Alma's office. The beer roaches. I closed my eyes so that I didn't have to watch them scatter.

"One day I'm going to leave this all behind," I said, as I took off my shoes. I flipped them over so that the roaches couldn't get inside. "The roaches, the beer, everything."

Sometimes I wondered if people chose their paths, or if we all acted out some pre-programmed code, like the boiler in the basement of Alligator. A few twists of a wrench, a couple knocks of a hammer, and then tick, tick, tick, until we all stopped. The funny thing was, I bet that spoiled boy who found the winning beer would've killed for my job. A chance to work on the Brewing Cloud, at one of its most renowned breweries? But I hated brewing. The noise of the boiler rattled my teeth and the smell of hot grain made me nauseous. To be honest, I didn't even like beer. It hurt my stomach.

I went to the kitchen and opened my mini-fridge. Inside, I saw half a stick of butter, a dozen eggs, and some week-old bologna. I took the butter and eggs out of the fridge and put a slab of butter on the camping stove. Then I remembered it'd been broken for days. I put the eggs and the butter back in the fridge, but I'd already cut a strip of butter to grease the pan, and I didn't want to waste it. I ate that, washed down with a big glass of rusty tap water. Then I ate a few slices of bologna and went to bed.

In the week that followed, two more codes were found, both by non-locals. One was by a man named Portlucky Johnson. He appeared on the news with his round belly and turned up nose and combed-over hair, a thick cigar between his teeth.

"It was a matter of statistics," he said, pawing at the

lapels of his navy blazer. "Of course, Dr. Wunder doesn't release his production statistics, but based on the size of the brewery I estimated that he released around fifty thousand bottles this week. I only needed to buy five hundred for a one percent chance at winning."

"And how many did you buy?" the reporter asked.

"Four thousand, one hundred, and sixty," he said, waving his cigar. "A twenty thousand dollar investment for just over an eight percent chance. Not high, but not bad. I had my wife buy another four thousand."

"Is she here to celebrate with you?" the reporter asked.

Portlucky looked surprised. "She went home to take care of the children," he said. He looked into the camera and waved. "Hello, Violet," he said. "Hello, Frankie. Hello Jane. I imagine they're quite proud of their daddy."

"And will they be coming up next month to see you receive your recipe?" the reporter asked.

Portlucky shuddered. "Oh no," he said. "The kids have school. And the expense to get them up here doesn't make sense."

The fourth winning bottle was found by a man named Phillip James Philip, a scholar from Venus.

"I respect my colleague, Mr. Portlucky Johnson, but I couldn't disagree with him more about statistical probability," Phillip said. He was a hunched man with piercing emerald eyes. But he spoke quickly and would barely make eye contact with the camera, so you couldn't really see them. He kept his shoulders hunched and his fingers steepled, their tips tapping against one another. He looked ready to run away at any moment. "For me, it was sheer improbability. We'd need to call it luck. Chance. If you divide the number of—"

"What Dr. Wunder recipe are you hoping to get?" the reporter asked.

The man, still staring at the ground, shivered with excitement. "Not an easy question," he said. "Of course, you must know that several years ago Dr. Wunder isolated a yeast strain called Torulaspora, which is among the things that makes an apple taste like an apple. When Torulaspora ferments, it creates apple-like aromatics. He put that yeast into a beer and laid it down in apple whiskey barrels, and the result was Apples Three Ways. The most popular beer on the Cloud. The Rare Release, *Apples Four Ways*, is the highest rated beer of the year."

"So you want Apples Four Ways?" the reporter said.

"Oh yes," Phillip said. "When I open my brewery, I'll serve each beer with a Wyndham apple slice from the Asteryx Colony. *Apples Five Ways!* Can you imagine?"

That left only one winning beer. After work that day, I didn't want to stay around Brewery Row and deal with the tourists, so I made my way to the Promenade. It's up behind Green Smoke and the route ain't easy. Even when the Cloud gets busy, it stays pretty quiet. From the stone walls you can see practically every brewery on the surface.

I sat down on one of the walls and watched as transport boats brought more tourists to the Cloud. I wanted to like them but I hated their entitlement, hated the way they trashed my home. Daddy, bless his heart, would've had a few choice words for the ones throwing up.

As I sat there, an old man walked by, pushing a refrigerated handcart.

"Interest you in a drink?" he asked.

I looked at his menu: a few selections from Alligator,

two from Green Smoke, two from Crystal Tree, one from Vampire. And a Dr. Wunder *Crunchbar.*

"What are you doing up here?" I asked. "Ain't no one up here. Wouldn't you do better business down by the breweries?"

The old man shrugged. "I'm up here for the same reason as you, I guess," he said. "Can't stand all the chatter. Say, you look familiar. You work behind the bar at the Crow's Nest?"

"No," I said. "And I don't have any money."

"No worries," the man said. He reached into the handcart and got a *Crunchbar.* "You want to open it or should I?" he asked, holding up a bottle opener.

"I'm not taking your beer," I said.

"Sheesh," the man said. "Never seen a lady so upset to get a drink." When I didn't laugh, he said, "Tell you what. I win, we sell the recipe and split the money. What do you think?"

I looked out over the docks. I closed my eyes as he fitted the cap into the opener. There was a sharp hiss as the bottle opened.

"Anything?" I asked, but I already knew the answer. There hadn't been any yelling, no noise that would've indicated a geyser of gold liquid.

"Sorry, kid," the old man said.

He handed me the beer. When I didn't take it, he set it on the stone wall beside me and walked away.

As soon as the man was out of earshot, I cried. Big fat tears and ropes of snot poured from my face. I hated the way I'd treated that vendor. I hated my life. Every time I tried to stop sobbing, I thought of my stupid stove, or the beer roaches, and that started a whole new wave of tears. Life didn't seem fair. Life *wasn't* fair. The thing that really got me, the thing that blew the waterworks wide open, was that I couldn't do anything about it.

"I miss you, Daddy," I said. Back when he'd been alive, things hadn't been so bad. Sure, we only had a little food, but at least we'd had each other. But then he'd collapsed at work and within a week he was gone. I stood and pressed my knees against the cold, hard stone. I knew that it'd leave dust marks on my pants but I didn't care. In the distance, I saw transport ships, and another cloud puttering past. I looked down.

Every once in a while, I read about someone who threw themselves over the edge of the Cloud. Everyone thought of beer as a beautiful, fun thing. I knew differently. Beneath the sweet surface, beer was like everything else: hard and ugly and mean. It drank people up and spit them back out. I climbed up onto the wall and closed my eyes.

"You're not having a good day," said a familiar voice from behind me. "Want to talk about it?"

I turned. Behind me stood the drink vendor.

"Go away," I said. "You don't know me."

Instead of leaving, the man sat on the stone wall and swung his legs over the side. "All the better," he said, patting the wall beside him. "We've never met and I doubt we'll ever meet again. You can tell me anything."

He had a point. I sat down and wiped my nose. "I'm a failure," I said, after a while. "I don't have any friends. My apartment is falling down around me and I can hardly afford food."

"That doesn't sound fun," the man said.

"No," I said. "And worst of all, I don't see any way out.

Like, my entire paycheck goes toward food and rent. It's not like I'm putting anything away so that I can afford a better situation. What do you do, in a situation like this?"

"You're asking me?"

"Sure."

"Well, I suppose you could ask for help," the man said. "I've always found that if your heart's in the right place, people will generally help. Like, here." He reached into his pocket and pulled out a black leather wallet. "You said you couldn't afford food. Here's a hundred dollars."

He held the bill toward me. I didn't take it.

"Ah," he said. "There's the problem." He let go of the bill and it fluttered over the edge of the Cloud.

"No!" I shouted, watching as the bill tumbled into space. That was a hundred dollars: a new stove, food for three weeks. "What'd you do that for?"

"You want help or you don't," the man said. "There's no in-between."

"But . . . I can't take your money," I spluttered.

"Then I'll just throw it over the edge," the man said, fishing another hundred from his wallet.

"Don't do that!" I plucked the bill from his fingers.

"Now you won't go hungry for a bit," he said. "That's good."

I felt the crumbled bill against my palm. "I can't live on charity forever," I said.

"And it's good you realize that," the man said. "But for now, until you get yourself into a more stable position, you need help. And when someone offers it, you shouldn't refuse."

"Fine," I said. "So what do I do next?"

"Do you have a job?"

"I keep the boiler running at Alligator Brewing. It doesn't pay much."

"Then you need a raise. Or get a new job."

"All right," I said, quietly.

"It's easy to despair," the man said. "One thing you can bet is that everyone you've ever met has felt despair. Even the ones who look like they've got everything. And each of us might be there again. But as you get older, you learn how to deal with it. You start learning that, and I know your life will change for the better."

"Thank you," I said.

"If I leave you alone, will you jump?" the man asked.

"If I jump, I can't ask for a raise," I said.

"Good girl," the man said. He patted my shoulder and got to his feet. "I'm getting too old to make the walk up here. But it's one of my favorite spots on the Cloud. Has been ever since I was a boy. Always quiet, hardly any tourists. And you can't beat the view."

"Wait," I said, as the man walked away. "You're from here?"

He didn't reply.

"Stop," I said. "What's your name?"

Again, he didn't answer.

I knew I was on the right track before the words left my mouth. "Dr. Wunder?" I said.

He rounded the corner and disappeared.

The next day, when I told Ms. Alma about the roaches, she got the saddest look on her face. She not only gave me a raise, but told me I could sleep in her guest room until I found a better place. And then she helped me find an apartment. I thought I didn't have any friends, but Ms. Alma came through for me, as did Bill, and the rest of the staff at Alligator pitched in to buy me a new stove. Then someone talked about me to Anne Westing, the hop farmer who'd won one of Dr. Wunder's rare recipes, and she offered me a job at her new brewery on Venus. I considered it carefully, but in the end, I decided to stay. The Brewing Cloud was my home.

Of course, someone won the fifth recipe. I don't know who it was and I didn't care to watch the news. During the contest, the excitement and the coverage made it easy to worry about someone else's life, but my experience on the Promenade made me realize I needed to care about my own. And now, against all odds, I'm happy.

Perhaps the only thing about my life that hasn't changed is that sometimes I still walk up to the Promenade. I sit on the stone wall and dangle my feet over the edge. Sometimes, I sit alone. Sometimes, other people join me. We talk about beer, or politics, or life. And every time, I secretly hope I'll hear that slightly accented voice: "You're not having a good day. Want to talk about it?"

I've never seen that man again, but darn if he wasn't right about everything.

The Rat Problem

Despite his sandy blonde hair, a hint of stubble, and a smile that had won "Best on the Brewing Cloud," Mike LaRose didn't have a partner. This, despite the fact that he was pleasant and kind. This, despite the fact that he owned Cloudship, one of the hottest breweries around. The only woman that had ever kept his attention had been Mona, but she was long gone.

Still, the day haunted him. He remembered playing poker with Mona, Captain Robot, and Bageera, waiting for Mr. Smooth to come back from the bathroom and make his bet. After ten minutes, when he hadn't returned, Captain Robot went after him. When he hadn't been in the bathroom, he and Captain Robot had tracked him to the inside of a dormant volcano, where Mr. Smooth was being forced to perform at a private birthday party. Mike, Captain Robot, and Mr. Smooth had walked out alive. Mona hadn't.

Mike shook his head and unlocked his motorcycle from its rack in the alley beside his home. It didn't help to dwell on the past. He swung a leg over the bike. With a flick of his wrist, he revved his engine and shot into the Cloud's wide streets. He was headed to Juniper, the latest of haunts. The dive bar had darts, and pool, and lots of single ladies. Plus, you got a free personal pizza with every drink order. It was hard to beat that.

He revved the engine again as he pulled to a stop outside the bar, scaring the women who stood out front. He locked his bike and went inside, instantly surrounded by warmth and noise and the smell of melting cheese. At the bar, he got a lager. A woman stood near the dart board with blonde hair and slender legs. It was Mona. His heart skipped a beat. That wasn't possible. Mona was dead.

The woman saw him staring and smiled, and her smile made her look so much like Mona that Mike blacked out. At least, that what's he thought happened. One minute he was at the bar, drinking a lager, and the next he was outside, unlocking his motorbike. He thought about heading up to the Promenade but he needed to be home, away from the lights and loud noises, away from the woman who looked like Mona and her haunting smile.

Horns blared as he weaved through traffic. He realized he was crying. When he got home, he stumbled into the house and pulled out a bottle of Cloudship *Motor Oil*. It was an American Barleywine, 15.8 percent alcohol by volume.

Mike drank. He drank and cried and drank a little more. Halfway through the bottle he realized he was singing "New Energy" by The Spacedogs at the top of his lungs. He was a big guy, but alcohol had always affected him. "Two Beer Mike," they'd called him in high school.

"I still sing your songs when I've had a few," he yelled to the empty room, taking a swig from the bottle. Plum. Toffee. Raisins. A little salt from the dried tears on his cheeks. "I know you do, too. But I've found someone new."

Someone new. He caught a look of himself in the mirror. His hair was matted and he wasn't wearing a shirt. When had that come off? He still clutched the bottle of *Motor Oil*.

"You're drunk," he said. He took out his phone and opened the Listen dating app.

Are you ready to Listen? said the cartoon penguin that appeared in the center of the screen. It did a little jig. *Ringing,* it said, the text appearing under its webbed feet. *Ringing, ringing. Now connected. Mary.*

Mike sat down. He felt a little nauseous. He put the phone to his ear. "Hello?" he said.

"You're not a woman," said the person on the other line. "Next!"

Mike looked at his phone. The penguin reappeared.

Ringing, it said. *Ringing, ringing. Now connected. Jennifer.*

"I've always liked the name Mike," purred the voice on the other line.

Mike coughed and licked his dry lips. "Are you from the Cloud?"

"Yes. Are you?"

"Me too. I work in a brewery. I'm a brewer."

"A brewer on the Brewing Cloud. How unique. Next!"

Mike awoke with a splitting headache. He stumbled to the bathroom and gulped down some water and a couple Ibuprofens, and then crawled back to the living room. He found his phone wedged between the couch cushions.

"Oh my gosh," he said. "I'm in a bad state."

The phone rang. He didn't mean to answer, but he had to make it stop.

"Mike," said the voice on the other end of the line. "This is Emily. Not sure if you remember me but we matched last night. We had the most amazing conversation. I'm kidding, of course. You cried and told me about the woman you lost. Anyways, you also told me you could hit a silver dollar off a buck's forehead at a hundred yards. I need your help. Meet me at the west gate of Dr. Wunder's in an hour?"

"What?" Mike mumbled.

"Great," said Emily. "See you there."

It took Mike a full minute of staring at his phone before he realized what had happened. He'd gotten drunk. He'd opened the Listen app. And somehow, against all odds, he'd gotten a date. Only, it was in an hour. And his head was killing him . . .

Mike arrived at the west gate of Dr. Wunder's facility exactly on time. It was only once he'd gotten on his motorcycle that he realized he had no idea what Emily looked like, but he shouldn't have worried. The west side of Dr. Wunder's was nothing more than a high wall that ran the length of the sidewalk, and only one woman stood near the gate.

"You're Mike," she said, as he pulled up. She had sharp green eyes and long brown hair. She wore a white gown. "I was fifty-fifty on whether you'd show. Come on."

Emily turned and stepped through the gate into Dr. Wunder's Magical Medicinal Brewery and Beer Emporium. He rubbed his eyes, just to make sure he wasn't hallucinating. He wasn't.

"What are you doing?" he said. "You can't go in there." He wanted to follow but he couldn't. This wasn't a minor case of trespassing. This was treason. No one went inside Dr. Wunder's.

"Oh, I didn't tell you?" Emily said. "I'm Emily Wunder. Like, Dr. Wunder's daughter. I live here. Now get inside, before someone sees us."

Mike wheeled his bike inside and Emily closed the gate behind him. They stood in a courtyard filled with box hedges organized into perfect, manicured shapes. There was a crocodile, its ivy tail sweeping up the smooth gray bark of a beech tree. A green vampire with red begonias for eyes. A puffy hedge that looked like green smoke.

"It's all the breweries on the Cloud," Mike said. "Crocodile Brewing. Vampire. Green Smoke."

"Yes," Emily said. "My dad's passion project. Personally, I think it's tacky. There's a Cloudship one over there." She pointed. "But come on. I'll show you how you can help."

Emily led him through a cloister, beneath a row of pillared archways. Mike saw rows of beehives, the tiny insects buzzing cheerfully. He smelled honeysuckle. Beyond the garden was a wide field. Perhaps a hundred yards distant, at the edge of the field, ran a line of pine trees. Between the trees at the edge of the field was a creature. Mike had never seen anything like it. It walked on all four legs and was covered in mousy gray fur. It had red eyes and had a thin, whip-like tail that trailed behind it like a snake.

"It looks like a rat," Mike said. "But . . . huge."

Emily nodded. "I was experimenting with a new growth hormone to grow bigger, juicier hops," she said. "But rats got into the feed."

"You have a giant rat problem," Mike said. "And you want me to kill them. You didn't want to call an exterminator?"

"I didn't want a stranger in the brewery," said Emily. "That's why I wanted you. You own Cloudship, right? You're another brewer. We've got a code. You know, 'Ne'er shall—'"

"I know the code," Mike said. "Ne'er shall one speak of another's operations, on loss of honor and the enmity of thine peers."

"There you go. You're not going to talk about anything you see here."

"I see," Mike said. "So this isn't a date."

Emily shrugged. "Let's see how it goes," she said. "Want to get some guns?"

Mike followed Emily through an arched door and down a set of stairs. They wound through a maze of corridors so tortuous that Mike had no idea which direction they were headed. All he knew was that they were going down. Down they went, deep into the bowels of the brewery. Occasionally Mike saw through a window or into an open door. There were bedrooms and bathrooms, kitchens and dens, but also strange and wondrous sites. One room appeared to be filled with rapidly multiplying cupcakes. In another, chickens were laying golden eggs. There was a room full of exploding marbles, another filled with chattering squirrels, and one where the floor burned with green flame.

Emily caught him looking. "This is where most of our research and development happens," she said. "I'm in charge of these floors. In that one there, we're developing a bottomless beer. It's not quite bottomless yet, but you get two or three refills before the glass blows up. We're still working on it." She traced her fingers along three lengthy gouges in the wall. "This is where the rats got out. Caused quite a bit of damage before we funneled them into the garden. And this . . ." They stopped in front of a large wooden door. Emily fished a skeleton key out of her pocket and dipped it into the lock. The key turned without a sound. "Welcome to the Armory," she said, pushing open the door.

The room ran as far as Mike could see. At even intervals down its lengths were rows of every weapon imaginable. There were guns, knives, flails, and maces, as well as glass orbs filled with different colored liquid. There were sticks of dynamite, and grenades, and something that looked like a Venus flytrap inflated to three times its size and stuffed with a bloated pufferfish. There were strange boxes marked with arcane symbols and, in a large clearing, an honest-to-god tank.

Mike whistled. "Are you planning for a war down here?" he asked.

"My father has a lot of enemies," Emily said. "But you never know when rats might get into your growing agent. Better to anticipate every eventuality than be caught off guard. That's something my father says."

"I suppose that makes some sort of sense," Mike said, scratching his beard. "Though this really seems like overkill." Emily led him past a line of spears to a wall that held hunting rifles.

"Take your pick," she said. "Ammunition is in that safe."

Mike walked down the line. There was a generous selection of varmint rifles, but having seen the size of the rat in the garden, Mike moved toward the larger caliber weapons. He needed something that could take down deer. That could stop an elk.

"This'll do," he said, lifting a weapon from its stand.

"I'd tell you that's a good choice but I really have no idea," she said. "I'm the R and D girl. Weapons are my father's bag."

"It'll do," Mike said, again. "You ready?"

They walked back to the garden that overlooked the tree line. The rat was still there, pawing at the ground.

"How many are there?" Mike asked.

"Three. I kept the others contained."

"Got it," Mike said. He propped the gun against the wall and looked down the sights. "Before I take this shot, there's something you should know. Just as I'm keeping your secrets,

I expect you to keep mine. I don't know what I told you when I was drunk, but I don't like to talk about my shooting. I was good at it once and I'd like to leave it behind me. Got it?"

Emily nodded.

"Also, if you want to go on another date, I'd be much obliged."

He fired, the gun jerking softly as it sent a high caliber bullet flying toward Emily's accidental creation. It took the creature through the base of the skull, severing the spinal cord and killing it instantly. The rat dropped without a sound. But from behind it, just beyond the trees, came a yelp of pain.

"What was that?" Mike asked.

He looked at Emily, her eyes wide. Then she was running down the lawn.

"Oh no," Emily said, as she ran. "Oh no, oh no, oh no."

Mike followed her, his heart sinking. He'd broken rule number one of responsible gun ownership: always know what was behind your target. And indeed, just beyond the tree line, a body lay in the grass. It belonged to a man who wore a blue suit, a white carnation pinned to his lapel.

"Father," Emily whispered.

He was dead. The bullet had gone straight through his left eye. From the look of the basket nearby, he'd been picking mushrooms.

"Oh my god," Mike said, staring at Dr. Wunder's body. He'd just killed Dr. Gustav Wunder, greatest brewer on the Cloud.

"Quickly," Emily said. "Follow me."

Before he could say anything else, Emily was on the move again, her long white dress flapping behind her as she ran back up the lawn.

"Emily," he said, pelting after her. "Wait. We should call an ambulance. Call the police."

But Emily didn't stop. She led him back into the house, back through the maze of corridors that led to her father's armory. She ran down the rows of weapons and stopped at a sleek metal pistol.

"My father always said that if he died, I needed to find this gun," Emily said. She lifted the weapon and turned a dial on the side. The green crystal atop the weapon blinked twice. "Cassiopeia," she muttered. "Green. Blue. Yes."

She aimed at a nearby wall and fired. Mike clapped his hands to his ears but there was no noise. Instead, a shimmering blue portal opened in the wall.

"What ... what is that?" Mike asked. Instead of answering, Emily jumped through the portal. The surface broke to allow her passage and then closed behind her. Mike was alone.

"Emily?" Mike said. No one responded. "I think I'm still drunk," he said, and then he jumped after her. For a moment, he could only see blue light, and then he stood on a path of well-worn dirt, the edges lined with fir trees.

"On my sixth birthday, my father gave me an envelope with a note he made me memorize," Emily said, staring down the path. She recited the poem: "The day I die in garden green, shot down by handsome, strong, and lean . . . the bullet gone straight through my head . . . this gun will raise me from the dead. Set the settings, set and true . . . on Cassiopeia, green, and blue . . . then give the gun to strong and lean and fire to the fire scene." She looked at Mike. "I think I'm supposed to give you the gun."

"Me?" Mike said. "Haven't I done enough?"

Emily shrugged. "You're the one who shot him, so you

must be strong and lean. Here, it's not heavy."

Mike took the gun. Like Emily said, it was lighter than he'd expected. The grip was smooth and cold and the crystal atop the gun blinked furiously.

"What do I do?"

Emily shrugged again. "The poem just said, 'Fire to the fire scene.' Try shooting."

Mike pointed the gun at the ground and fired. Once again, a shimmering blue portal in the ground. Just beyond its liquid surface, Mike saw a field filled with . . . yes, those were hops. And what looked like barley. The crops were being harvested. And they were . . . screaming?

"Hops!" said a stalk of barley, as it was cut down by a man with a scythe. "I love you!"

"I love you too, barley," said a bine of hops.

"Fire again," Emily said. "I don't think that's what we want."

Mike took another shot. The portal opened and a giant, serpentine head poked through, gnashing its jaws and spraying Emily with green saliva.

"Okay, again," Emily said. "Again!"

Mike fired. The new portal opened to a lake of lava. On the shore of the lake, just inside the portal, was a rowboat.

"This must be the fire scene," Emily said, as a popping bubble sent a jet of flame into the air. "Maybe we could go on a romantic boat ride. Mike?"

He looked like a scared puppy. He stood rigid, his hands clenched at his sides. His eyes were wide and a sheen of sweat stood out from his forehead. "You said fire scene," he whispered. "Not lava. Fire."

"Mike?" Emily said, again. She put a hand on his

shoulder. "What's going on?"

Mike shook. "Before I was a brewer, I was a bodyguard for Mr. Smooth. My partner Mona and I were the best in the business. We had a show on Kepler-78 and Mr. Smooth got kidnapped. Someone wanted to make him perform at a birthday party. Guy had a house built into a volcano. We all went in to save him—me, Captain Robot, Mona. We rescued Mr. Smooth, but Mona . . . she didn't make it."

"Oh Mike," Emily said. "I'm sorry."

"The last I saw her, she was slipping beneath the lava," he said. "She'd been shot. That's when I retired. Thought the brewing life would change things. I said I'd never pick up another gun. Now I have and I've killed Dr. Wunder."

Emily rubbed his shoulder. "You shouldn't worry about my father," she said. "He's a special man. If this happened . . . well, I can only assume it's because he wanted it. I can't really explain it but it seems he always has a plan."

She took his hand and a shiver of electricity ran through him. Her skin was soft. This close, he could smell her clean, earthy scent, like warm asphalt after a heavy rain.

"Come on," she said. "We can help him. If it's any consolation, I don't think this is actually lava. Don't you think we would've felt it by now?"

She was right. Although they stood near the lake's surface, Mike couldn't feel the waves of heat that should've been radiating from it.

"All right," Mike said. "Let's do this."

Emily stepped into the little rowboat and Mike climbed in after her. The boat slid into the lake and Mike picked up the oars.

"I was in love once, too," Emily said, as Mike rowed.

"His name was Brett. We met while I was studying abroad in Florence. We used to meet in cafés and he'd recite Romantic poetry. Or read to me in Italian. He was American but he had a terrific Italian accent."

"Sounds . . . fun?" Mike said.

"It was, until we broke up. The strange thing was, there was nothing in particular that happened. No big fight or anything. We just grew apart. I kept thinking we might get back together, but he got married two years ago. He's happy, I think. I don't know."

"I suppose it's a little less dramatic, though I imagine it's still painful," Mike said. He rowed until they reached the other side of the lake. On the shore was a pedestal, and beside that was a basket, and a granite coffin. Emily got out of the boat and opened the basket. It was filled with feathers and bits of bone. She closed the lid and lifted a piece of parchment from the pedestal.

"There's another poem here," she said. "If Dr. Wunder is lost or dead, place these feathers on your head. Spin once, spin twice, spin thrice, fall down while wearing feathers as a crown. Wave your hands, sing and clap, chant the words to bring him back. Eekoonay, eekoonay, shablagoo. And while one chants, the other, too. Eekoonay, eekoonay, shablagum—keep chanting till the deed is done."

"That's it?"

"That's it." She opened the basket again. "So here, put these feathers on your head."

Mike took a step back. "I'm not touching those," he said. "They look sticky."

"They are sticky. And you're the one who killed my dad, so . . . feathers."

Mike took the feathers and stuck them to his head. "I don't understand," he said. "What is this going to do?"

Emily shrugged. "No idea," she said. "When it comes to my father, I don't ask questions."

Mike sighed. "Eekoonay, eekoonay, shablagoo," he said. It sounded ridiculous. "You want me to keep chanting?"

"That's what the poem said," she said. "Keep it going, but with a little gusto." Mike repeated the words and Emily joined in. "Eekoonay, eekoonay, shablagum," she said. "Eekoonay, eekoonay, shablagum."

The two of them were chanting for half a minute before the top of the coffin slid off and Dr. Wunder stepped out. He was as solid as the rocks at their feet, as alive as the daughter who yelped with joy and wrapped her arms around him. He hugged her back. He looked radiant, with glowing skin and bright eyes, a thick mane of brown hair streaked with white. His clothes were pressed and expertly tailored. A gold pocket watch hung from his waist.

"Excellent timing," he said, looking at the watch. "My dear Emily, I'm so glad to see you. And Mr. LaRose! How wonderful. I'm a big fan of Cloudship—those IPAs are delightful."

"Dr. Wunder," Mike said. "How are you . . . I'm sorry about . . ."

Dr. Wunder waved him off. "Think nothing of it. Accidents happen. I'm sorry I can't say more, but I hope you know it's for the greater good. All will be revealed in time."

Emily rolled her eyes.

"And now, if you could take us home?" Dr. Wunder continued. "Mike, set the gun to Blue, Green, Stalwart. That should get us back to the garden."

Acknowledgements

No book is written in a vacuum, unless it's literally written inside a vacuum, in which case your friends, family, and co-workers would probably forgive you for skipping the acknowledgements in lieu of getting out of what seems like a really dangerous situation.

Anyways, this book wasn't written in a vacuum.

I owe a great debt to my family, particularly my mom and dad (to whom this work is dedicated), as well as my grandmothers, Judy Napp and Rose Gould, who always encouraged me to write. Scott Gould, Lara Gould, and Kim Gould had to live with me growing up, so there's that. Maisa Gould and Cam Fry have never shared a house with me, but I've always benefitted from their unwavering support.

Rachel Falik aka Dr. Banana was the spark that made me dust off this old manuscript, which I began as part of my MFA thesis project at Chatham University. Rachel has believed in me since the day we met and continues to support me and my writing.

Our cat Crumb deserves a shout out for continuously providing comic relief. If you see a Star Wars creature scratching at my books and running around our house with full loaf of bread in her mouth, that's actually Crumb.

A big thank you goes to the people directly involved in the creation of this work, which includes my editor, John

Knight, as well as my amazing cover artist, Ryan Hayes, and my interior designer, fellow yinzer Stewart Williams.

Sam Taylor, Rob Corradetti, Yeye Weller, and Kailah Ogawa didn't help with this particular project, but I find their work inspiring. The same goes for Roald Dahl, Stephen King, and Kurt Vonnegut, my literary mentors, as well as Radiohead, Strange Ranger, Ratboys, Kamasi Washington, Pinegrove, The Hotelier, and PUP, who provided the soundtrack to this work.

Hop Culture Managing Editor John Paradiso and Head of Partnerships Grace Weitz are the best co-workers a person could ask for, and genuinely two of the nicest people I've ever met.

My friends Phil Greenblatt, Meredith Wolfe, Levi Wolfe, Amie DiTomasso, Dave Menasche, Nic Pabon, Lissy Petrozza, and Leslie Phillipsie kept me sane throughout the writing process, which is actually a really hard job.

Last but not least, a huge thank you to the beer community, which has supported me and Hop Culture since we joined its ranks in 2017.

Stay juicy!

About The Author

KENNY GOULD is a graduate of Duke University and the Founder and Editor in Chief of Hop Culture, a daily online magazine covering the craft beer industry. He used to be a staff writer at *Gear Patrol Magazine*, and has also contributed to *Bon Appetit, Men's Health, Time Out New York, Thrillist,* and *Vice,* among others. He's currently a food and beverage contributor at *Forbes.*

He likes his job a lot.

Connect with him on Instagram at @hopculturemag or via email at kenny@hopculture.com.

Printed in Great Britain
by Amazon

57096402R00073